THE GIRL WHO WASN'T THERE

BOOKS BY THOMAS B. DEWEY

The "Mac" series:

Draw the Curtain Close
Every Bet's a Sure Thing
Prey for Me
The Mean Streets
The Brave, Bad Girls
You've Got Him Cold
The Case of the Chased and the Chaste
The Girl Who Wasn't There
How Hard to Kill
A Sad Song Singing
Don't Cry for Long
Portrait of a Dead Heiress
Deadline
Death and Taxes
The King Killers
The Love-Death Thing
The Taurus Trip

The Pete Schoefield Series

And When She Stops
Go To Sleep, Jeannie
Too Hot For Hawaii
The Golden Hooligan
Go, Honeylou
The Girl With The Sweet Plump Knees
The Girl in the Punchbowl
Only on Tuesdays
Nude in Nevada

The Singer Batts Series

Hue and Cry
As Good As Dead
Mourning After
Handle with Fear

Others Novels

My Love Is Violent
Hunter at Large
Can a Mermaid Kill?
A Season of Violence

THE GIRL WHO WASN'T THERE

THOMAS B. DEWEY

WILDSIDE PRESS

CHAPTER ONE

Barry Henley's widow was an excessively attractive brunette of petite bulk and large magnetism. She gave an impression of bearing herself like a precious gift in her own hands. Also, at this time she was frightened, and the measures she took to hide the fact only made it more obvious: the over-reaching way she dug out a cigarette and overgraciously allowed me to light it; the vivid smile when the ritual was accomplished; the indirect chatter for a while, as if she had just dropped in to renew a casual acquaintance.

Still, I had a feeling of being honored that she had come. In another client this might have been calculated to serve her advantage, but in Virgie Henley it was to be taken for granted.

"It's been a long time," I said.

"Almost a year, Mac. How are you anyway?"

"Fine.

In the lull that followed, I mixed her a drink. She held the glass in both hands, sitting tentatively in the big chair. You could have set three of her in it and had room left over. I watched her red mouth at the glass and her tiny fingers and the fragility of her fully endowed but almost miniature body and wondered how she had managed to live to her present age, which I guessed to be all of twenty-three.

"Tastes good," she said, smiling over the glass. "I've been mostly on the wagon. For a while right after—it happened, I was drinking quite a lot. It doesn't really help but it seems to."

"I guess so. You look great, if I may say so."

"You're sweet to say so."

"Still working for the same firm?"

She nodded.

"The old alma mater—Brangwyn and Schwartz, LaSalle Street's fin-est."

It was a brokerage firm where she had worked before she married Barry. She quit then, but it hadn't been much of a vacation. They had been married less than a year when Barry died.

The sudden demise of a colleague is always disturbing, if only because it reminds us once again that we live on the edge of disaster and who knows much about tomorrow? Even though I had known Barry Henley and his wife only casually, I still remembered the announcement of his end. It had come to me by radio in the anonymous voice of a local newscaster.

"The body of Barry Henley, a private investigator, was found early this evening in a west side alley. Police are looking into the possibility of homicide, although outward appearances indicate that Henley was the victim of an accident. His neck was broken, apparently as the result of a fall from a high building.

"Mrs. Henley, wife of the victim, stated she did not know what her husband was working on at the time of his death."

Because we had met a few times and I had given Barry some advice, and because I remembered Virgie Henley as little more than a kid, I had called by telephone to offer help if she needed it. I had sent flowers and I had called briefly and formally on the occasion of the modified wake for Barry. That had been almost a year before.

"Barry thought so much of you," Virgie was saying. "He used to say, 'If I ever got in the kind of trouble I couldn't take to the cops, I'd go to Mac.'"

I moved in my creaky chair. It was always nice to hear, but she had such an intensity in her lovely little face!

"He didn't like the kind of work he had to do mostly," she said. "Domestic relations and skip tracing, you know? He always felt sort of degraded."

"He was young," I said. "Didn't he ever try for the civil police?"

"Yes, he tried. He had a physical disability. Funny, it didn't keep him out of the army but it kept him out of the police." She sipped at her drink. "You were on the force, weren't you?"

"Yes."

"Barry used to say, 'He must have been railroaded out. If it wasn't for being a Scotchman—that's the only trouble with him, he ain't Irish.'"

I laughed.

"Look, you're running me in debt here. Suppose you tell me your troubles and put me to work?"

"Troubles—? Oh, the reason I came. Maybe I'm just silly. Promise not to laugh?"

I raised my right hand solemnly and she told me the story.

* * * *

I didn't laugh. I made her another drink and walked around the desk a couple of times and sat down again.

"Let's be sure I've got it straight," I said. "First the fellow about the insurance thing—said he was checking on an old policy of Barry's. You went to see if you could find any such policy."

"I looked everywhere."

"And you don't know how much of the apartment this fellow might have covered while you were looking."

"Probably all of it. I didn't give it a thought till he suddenly appeared in the bedroom, where the desk is."

"You didn't find any policy?"

"No, and I couldn't remember ever hearing of one."

"Then he said maybe it was a mistake in the records and went away?"

"Yes."

"That was a week ago. Three days later came the lady who claimed to be from the assessor's office."

"That's right. I was horribly stupid. I didn't ask her a single question. I let her in and showed her everything in the place. Finally I got to thinking she was pretty nosy for an assessor and I guess she sensed it. Anyway she kind of hurried and got out."

"And when you checked with the assessor's office, you found they had no people out at that time."

"Yes."

"And yesterday two men claimed to be maintenance men employed by the owner of the building and wanted to look the apartment over for purposes of repair and redecoration."

"On them I drew the line. I said I was unable to let them in and they would have to come back later."

"How much argument did they put up?"

"They argued but they didn't get ugly about it."

"Did they show you any credentials, like a work order, estimate sheet?"

"No. They just kept saying this was the only time they could inspect the place and if I didn't let them do it, I wouldn't get any redecorating or repair work done and would have to pay for it myself. I said that was the way it would have to be then."

"And the reason you didn't let them in was because of these previous mysterious visitors?"

"Yes. My little brain finally got suspicious."

"These two yesterday—they didn't give you any trouble, make any threats?"

"No. They argued awhile, then gave up."

I thought about it. Virgie watched me too expectantly.

"You didn't recognize any of these people? Never saw them before?" I asked.

"No. I'm positive."

"Have you thought of anything they might have been after?"

"I tried, but I can't think of a thing. Certainly not money. I thought of jewels or something, but I've cleaned the place thoroughly at least three times in the last year. I'm sure I'd have noticed anything like that."

"Did Barry confide in you much about his work?"

"No, he was very close-mouthed about it. He was quite a talker about other things, but his work was confidential. A lot of it was, well, kind of sordid I guess, and he didn't like to tell me about it. He had strong opinions about women; there were nice women and there were the others. He could get real mean about the others, but I was a nice woman so I was different."

After a moment she said, "Now what sent me off like that? I'm sorry. Go ahead, Mac."

I looked at my watch.

"You probably want to be getting home," I said. "I would like to look around your apartment myself, preferably by daylight. If you'll give me a key or arrange with the manager to let me in—you might wrap up anything personal and take it to work with you. Or if you'll set it aside and label it, I won't touch it."

She smiled ruefully.

"I don't have much to hide," she said. "I've been leading an awfully quiet life."

"The second thing—I'll set up a date for us to go over some mug shots."

"The police?" She winced. "Is it necessary?"

"Better sooner than later," I said. "If you should recognize even one of your callers, we'd be a big jump out in front."

"But nothing has really happened, Mac."

"We don't want anything to happen. We just want to go on living our stodgy, quiet, uneventful little lives."

She smiled then. "All right."

"Would you like me to go home with you now?"

"No," she said. "I'm sure nobody's following me. And I'm not afraid to be at home alone. I don't have to let anyone in. Besides, I've got Barry's gun, a .38 special."

"Barry teach you how to use it?"

"Yes. I'm a pretty good shot."

"I hope you won't hesitate if the need should arise."

"Don't worry."

"Have you talked to anyone else about this?"

"No—well, I told the manager of the building and told her not to let anyone in my apartment under any circumstances."

"That's all?"

"I told Paul Budge."

"Budge?"

"My attorney." She blushed. "Excuse me for sounding like a big shot. I mean, Mr. Budge took care of things for Barry sometimes and he was awfully helpful when Barry died and took care of Barry's files and all. I told him I was coming to see you."

"How did he take care of Barry's files?"

"Well, one of the first things the police wanted after Barry died was to go through his files. I called Paul, Mr. Budge, about it and he said absolutely not, not unless they came with warrants."

"Did he explain why?"

"He said there might be things in the files that would subject innocent people to embarrassment or even legal action if their records were opened up. He said it was sort of like a lawyer's files."

"What happened to the files?"

"We put them in storage. Paul came out to the apartment and helped me. There were three filing cabinets. One was empty—Barry was kind of optimistic. The other two had some files in them and a lot of supplies, paper and so on. We put everything into one cabinet and Paul pasted some stickers over each drawer to seal them, and I called a transfer company and put the cabinet in storage. I don't know why I thought I had to keep the files, but the storage doesn't cost much."

"Did Budge go through the files himself before they were sealed?"

"I don't think so; he wouldn't have had time. I asked him if he knew anything about Barry's cases that I ought to know, but he said there was nothing."

"What procedure do you have to go through to get at the files?"

"I have to sign them out, like a safe deposit box at a bank. Or Mr. Budge can get them out if anything should happen to me."

"Only if something happens to you?"

"Well, he has a power of attorney. I guess if I was sick or something—"

"Did Budge have any ideas when you told him about your strange visitors?"

"He seemed very puzzled. He asked me some questions and offered to come out and see me, but I said no. I can't really afford that much legal service." Again the great smile. "I don't know if I can afford you either, Mac."

"Don't be like that, Virgie. You can give me a hot market tip some day, right out of Brangwyn and Schwartz."

I picked up the telephone and got hold of a guy on the cops and told him we'd like to look at some pictures.

"Sure," he said, "but if you're reporting me a crime—"

"Nobody's hurt, not yet."

"Who's the client?"

I told him.

"Barry Henley's widow?"

"Right."

"Okay. Tomorrow? Five o'clock?"

I checked with Virgie and she said that would be all right. I thanked the guy and hung up.

"It's a drag," I said, "but it might pay off. Meanwhile, how do I get into your apartment?"

She opened her purse and came up with a key.

"I can borrow one from the manager," she said.

We went outside. She had a green and white, low-priced car a couple of years old, parked down the street. It was cold and a wind off the lake whipped at us. She tucked her hand under my arm.

"Thanks for everything, Mac," she said. "See you tomorrow?"

"Suppose you come over here after work. I'll drive you downtown."

"About a quarter to five."

I opened the door and she got in and got the motor going. She smiled through the window, waved and started off, heading for the Drive. I started back to the office.

A taxi pulled out of the street that dies just before running through my office and took a route following Virgie.

My own car was parked a few feet away. I ducked into it, managed a U-turn and joined the parade. When we got onto the crowded Drive, we were equally spaced: Virgie in front, then three cars, then the taxi, then three more cars and me.

At Diversey Parkway, the taxi left the Drive and doubled back toward the Loop. I stayed with it to Division and LaSalle and then in the rush-hour traffic, I lost it. I never did get a look at the fare, if any.

I brooded about it for a couple of hours and decided to let it go. I didn't want to give Virgie the jitters and I couldn't very well invite myself to spend the night with her. Besides, she had the gun.

Later, when I went to sleep, I didn't enjoy what you could call a real deep repose. It dreamed very bad. But at that time I didn't believe in dreams.

CHAPTER TWO

The next day I spent five fruitless hours examining Virgie's apartment. It was in an old building with tired cornices and frayed carpets in the halls, but Virgie's three rooms were lovingly decorated and spotlessly clean. I did as thorough a job as ever in my life. I emptied every kitchen cupboard and drawer and looked under the shelf linings. I went through a desk and the drawers of three occasional tables, paper by paper, box by box. I checked for false bottoms and backs. I took the bed apart and put it back together and looked under the cushions of every chair. There were quite a few books, mostly in a ceiling-high case in the living room, and I took down every book and made sure nothing had been hidden among the pages. There were some men's suits I took to be Barry's and I took them all down and felt carefully all over to see whether anything had been stuck under the linings. I looked under every rug and broke down every pile of linen and fabric. When I had exhausted all these possibilities, I rechecked the easier, more obvious places. It took me all of the five hours without a break, and when I finished I had nothing, absolutely nothing that could have any importance for anyone but Virgie.

* * * *

As I was unprepared to believe that Virgie had enemies or a colorful past, I was pretty well stuck with Barry himself as the pivot of the problem. But Barry was dead. With two hours to waste following the search, I paused at the Tribune Building and leafed back through the files to the date of Barry's "accident." It was a small story but it included an address.

West and a little south of the Loop, I left the car in an unoccupied loading zone and walked around for a while. According to the news story, Barry Henley had met his death in a certain alley behind a specific number on a certain street. I had to walk almost half a mile to establish the number, then backtrack around the corner and into a blind alley to get to the spot.

The ten-story canyon gave me vertigo as I looked up. At the top the two buildings seemed to lean to each other. The tiers of high, blank windows were slate-gray and unlabeled. But on the one building, beside a small service door on a metal plaque were the words: "B and D Hotel and Restaurant Supply Co."

It rang no bell. The woods were full of such. It didn't necessarily connect with Barry Henley at all. The firm could have been in that location ten days or ten years.

Opposite the restaurant outfit, an iron fire ladder crawled down the brick wall to within eight feet of the ground. I jumped, caught the bottom rung and pulled up hand over hand till I could get my feet on it. It was old and wobbly but well enough anchored. I climbed it, pausing at each floor to look through the windows, both the near ones past which I climbed and those across the way. On the third floor of the building I was scaling, I looked in on a dress factory. Women sat at long tables littered with fabric. One turned and looked at me without curiosity and went back to her work. Across the alley in the other building, the shades were drawn.

I assailed two more flights and saw nothing in either building. On the fifth floor of the restaurant supply firm was a warehouse jammed with kitchen and bar equipment: big stainless steel units along with bar stools, tables and a hundred other items of the food and liquor service industry.

This was repeated on the sixth floor, but with more variety. It was all very interesting but it didn't tell me anything. My hands were stiff on the cold rungs of the ladder. But I had got well past the point of no return and decided to go on up, on the hunch that there would be an easier way down inside the building.

At the eighth floor, peering between two rungs of the ladder, I rested and watched five Negroes in a stockroom shooting craps. One of them looked at me, went stiff and alerted the others. They all stared at me. I grinned cheerfully, waved at them and went on up.

At the ninth-floor level there was an iron grilled balcony about two feet wide. I eased over a hip-high rail onto it and leaned gratefully against a window, catching my breath and flexing my cold hands. I looked down over the rail, not without reluctance, and tingled unpleasantly from the back of my scalp to the pit of my stomach. It was a long, hard drop to the cold concrete, eighty or ninety feet below. A man who survived it would likely wish he hadn't. At the blind end of the alley was a loading platform. A pickup truck was drawn in under it. Two high corrugated steel doors were closed down.

Behind me, a dirty window gave on an empty loft. Without expectation, I gripped the bottom of the frame with my fingers and heaved lightly. The window rose, squeaking. So I had my way down on the inside.

I took another look down into the alley, then turned to crawl through the window opening. A light caught my eye across the way, on the ninth floor of the restaurant supply firm. It was a dim light and draperies at each side obscured some of the view. But I made out what seemed to be an apartment or showroom, with a couch, a couple of chairs, a table with a lamp. It could be the quarters of a night watchman or caretaker; or a private office of the establishment. It didn't signify much. But I kept looking, remembering the rail of the little balcony that would hit a man just low enough to flip him over, and the direct line of sight across the alley into the unexpected apartment.

An inner door opened over there and a woman came into the room. She was in flimsies, shoes and hose. She reached up, took down a slip and pulled it over her head. Next a dress, over the head quickly, then adjusting, smoothing it. She didn't bother with the usual feminine circumspection to avoid mussing the hairdo. In spite of the distance and the low light, I had seen her clearly enough to know she was young and shapely. I hadn't seen her face. But it was easy enough to see why she didn't bother about the hair. She didn't have any. She was bald as a mannequin.

Someone shouted. I looked down and a beat patrolman was gesturing vigorously with his stick. I waved at him. He went on gesturing to me to get the hell down from there. I waved again, turned around, raised the window another foot and climbed inside. By the time I found my way to the street, the policeman had disappeared.

I hung around the B and D Hotel and Restaurant Supply Co for about half an hour, watching the entrance. People came out and went in but none of them looked like the bald-headed lady. At four-thirty I gave it up and went home to keep my appointment with Virgie.

CHAPTER THREE

She arrived at ten minutes to five, breathless from the cold and from hurrying. We sat around for a few minutes before heading downtown. Her day and the night before had been as uneventful as my investigation of her apartment. I didn't mention my encounter with the bald one. It seemed ludicrous in retrospect.

On the way downtown I told her we would probably have to delve in Barry's files for a lead. She was willing.

"I'll go with you to sign them out," she said. "Maybe Paul Budge could help us."

"Maybe later," I said. "I'd like it to be just the two of us first time around."

"Whatever you say, Mac."

* * * *

We sat around a scarred table with Sergeant Monday and looked at pictures: females first because there were fewer of them, and there was a chance Virgie would spot a woman's face more readily than a man's. But whoever the woman was who posed as a tax assessor, either she had no record or Virgie couldn't find her.

Virgie got a little bleary and we sent out for coffee. The Sergeant had no cogent ideas about our problem. Nothing had been done that would give him a handle and the whole thing was nebulous.

"You only lived in that place about two years," he said. "Sometimes a fella will stash something in a place and say he sweats out a short rap, he'll come back or send somebody around to pick it up. You know after he gets out of stir, or maybe while he's in stir, somebody else gets wind of whatever he hid and they'll try to snitch it off him. I've seen 'em tear a place apart to find a sweepstakes ticket."

"I doubt that Barry ever bought a sweepstakes ticket," Virgie said, smiling at him so intensely that he ran his hand through his hair and got red in the face.

"I suppose not, ma'am; anyway, too much time would have gone by now. I was just makin' the point."

"I understand," Virgie said. "Shall we look at some more pictures?"

"Sure. Pictures we got."

The pages of the big book turned slowly. Time ticked away. Virgie did her best, but identified nobody. We drank a lot of coffee. The Sergeant was in and out. By seven-thirty, Virgie had her head propped on her hand. There was a limit to what could be done in a single sitting. After so many faces, they all begin to look alike. I had got up to move an adjournment when she turned a page, turned it back, studied it for a moment and said, "Wait a minute."

I leaned over her shoulder. Sergeant Monday came in and peered over her other shoulder. Virgie was pointing to a guy of around forty, not bad-looking, with a slight scar over his left eye, slick black hair and a rather long face.

"Who's that?" she said.

"Is he one of them?" I asked.

"I think so. One of the two who said they were estimating repairs on the apartment—the two I didn't let in."

Sergeant Monday looked at me over Virgie's head.

"Whisky Davis," he said.

"Whisky?" Virgie said. "What kind of a name is that?"

"Well, ma'am, that name got started because Davis has a bad throat. He talks like a whisky tenor, hoarse and funny-sounding."

"What does he do?" I asked.

"One of Brophy's boys," the Sergeant said. "You know Brophy."

"Not personally."

"One thing, he's got a restaurant supply business. B and D he calls it, over on the west side."

"Oh," I said. "Legitimate front?"

"Well, you know how it goes. Say you're opening a joint, you need some furniture and fixtures—Brophy will sell 'em to you. Make good terms and all. High interest. I don't know how his prices compare but I guess the stuff he sells is all right. Only Brophy is the type of operator that likes to close every deal. Say you decided you didn't want to buy from Brophy or wanted to look around first, Brophy is the type of fella that would shove his stuff down your throat. He has the hard boys to help him, you know?"

"In with the mob?" I said.

"Good enough to stay in business."

"He's a racketeer," Virgie said.

"Yes, ma'am he is."

"What in the world would he want with me?"

"That is a question," the Sergeant said, "that if it was me, I would want to find the answer."

"What else does Brophy have?" I asked him.

"Oh, this and that. He comes and goes. He's pretty careful. And then too, these people he pushes around, they won't complain much. We almost had Brophy on a real good beef once, but he slipped out."

"Where's his headquarters?"

"He stays mostly around his place of business. Got one of the upper floors fixed up in a couple of apartments. Then he has a big home out on the South Side, respectable neighborhood. I hear he has a wife out there."

"You remember Barry saying anything about Brophy?" I asked Virgie.

"No," she said.

"You don't remember Barry ever doing any work for a restaurant owner, anybody like that?"

"Unh-uh," she shook her head. "But as I told you, Barry didn't talk much about his work."

I looked at the Sergeant and he looked at me and we didn't strike any sparks. I gave Virgie a hand up.

"That's enough for tonight."

"I guess so," she said, "I can hardly see my hand in front of my face." She gave the Sergeant a smile and he blushed and ran his fingers through his stiff gray hair.

"Any time, ma'am," he said. "We're interested in crime prevention, too. This guy comes around again, give us a call."

"Thank you, Sergeant," she said.

We left and walked to my car and drove slowly out over the bridge and north on Michigan Avenue, drifting.

"Would you care to have dinner with an old man?" I asked.

She put her hand on my arm.

"You're the nicest old man I know," she said.

* * * *

Over the wreckage of a good meal on the near North Side, we pawed and worried at the problem.

"Question," I said. "How come they're so devious about it? If they're after something of great value, you being alone there and on the light side, why don't they just push in and take it?"

She watched me with her blue-green eyes out of the pale, lovely face under the blue-black hair.

"Possible answers," I said. "Number one: they're people of repute who can't risk involvement. Number two: if it's something they think may take a long time, they might go easy just to avoid arousing suspicion or extra obstacles.

"Like a violence against you, for instance, might open your apartment to investigation by the police. This would impede their search. In fact, the police might find it first—whatever it is."

"Yes," Virgie said. "Whatever it is. What do you think it is, Mac?"

"No idea. Tell me, this last job of Barry's—you told the papers you didn't know what it was. Was that true?"

"Is that what I told them? I might have said anything. I wasn't responsible. If that's what I said, it was true all right. I didn't know. Only this much, it was something big and unusual for Barry. He was real excited about it, I could tell. 'Baby,' he said, 'when this one is wrapped up, we'll be in the clear. We'll go!'"

"But he didn't tell you what it was?"

"No."

I thought about it.

"After that first request from the police for the files," I asked, "did they ever come back with a warrant?"

"No, they never did. They decided Barry had died by accident and I guess that settled it."

"Do you think it was an accident?"

She took time to find a cigarette and lean across for me to light it, then with that expectant look like a child's, her red lips twisting about the words, she said, "I don't know, Mac, I just don't know. I was getting so I didn't think about it any more when this—these people started coming around."

Her face began to come apart.

"Let's get out of here," I said.

* * * *

On the street in the cold evening, she held my arm tightly. The fresh air, or the moving or something, had braced her and she had all that wonderful poise working for her again. Her high heels made only the lightest tapping on the cement, and the touch of her gloved fingers was a bird's weight on my arm. She was incredibly small for a grown woman, but she had this immense style.

At my car, half a block from the restaurant, she hung back.

"Could we walk a little?" she said. "Anyway around the block?"

"Certainly."

She tied up the broken ends of our conversation.

"If it wasn't an accident," she said, "if Barry was murdered—what do you think it means?"

"I don't know. Did he ever mention having an enemy, a blood enemy, somebody who was out to get him?"

"No, but he wouldn't. As Barry used to say, he was a black Irish bum. He prided himself that he could take care of anything that might come up."

And at the; age of twenty-eight, I thought, he fell or was pushed off a brick wall ninety feet in the air, and he hadn't taken care of that now, had he?

"He was a great guy, Mac," Virgie said softly. "I loved him awfully."

I kept quiet and let her have it for as long as it would last. She was young. She would love again.

There might have been a little telepathy in the air.

"I have to be honest though," she went on. "I can't pretend my life ended when Barry died. But no matter what happens, I owe him so much! You see, I was brought up kind of—sheltered. I was really innocent. Barry was big and a little rough and sometimes impatient. But he knew some things weren't too easy for me. It's hard sometimes for overprotected girls to get used to actually living with a man. Barry understood this. He was gentle and sweet with me, without being soft, if you know what I mean. He made me love him and like it, you know?"

"I guess I know."

We moved a little faster. As if embarrassed by her frankness, she drew herself into a tighter, quicker stride.

"Excuse me," she said, "for getting into the story of my life. You make it too easy, Mac."

"Say whatever comes to mind. Something may help."

"It all helps. Just to talk about Barry helps."

"Have you stopped to think that maybe these visits you've been getting don't have anything to do with Barry?"

"Well—but what else?"

"Do you ever bring any work home from the office?"

"Brangwyn and Schwartz?" she laughed quietly. "No, never."

"Do you do anything for them of a confidential nature, anything outsiders would like to know about?"

"Oh, some things, but I'd be the last one to try to pump or anything. I don't know enough to be worth the trouble."

"Uh-huh," I said.

"It was at the office I met Barry. He was working for Dun and Bradstreet, you know, one of those jobs? I was a receptionist then. Barry used to kid around with me while he waited to see Mr. Schwartz. He scared me at first, but he had those Irish eyes and that sense of humor—he more or less swept me off my feet. But it wasn't easy. It took him a year to talk me into going steady. Then another year—sometimes I wonder why he put up with me so long."

"I don't wonder for five seconds."

She squeezed my arm.

"You're a sweet-talking guy, Mac," she said. "You know something, I was scared to death to come to your office. I thought, 'He'll just laugh at me. A man like that with the things he has on his mind. He'll laugh at me and send me home.'"

"I'm that spooky?"

"Not actually, not after a person gets to know you, but before—boy, I was shook. But I didn't know where else to go and Barry had this big admiration for you—"

Somewhere along in there, I had come in.

We made the circuit of the block. The street was quiet and the wind had died down. Virgie had regained her confidence, I thought, and it was a pleasure to be with her.

"You drove over from your office?" I asked her.

"Yes. I had to park half a block down the street."

"I'm sorry."

"Maybe it's just as well, in case—"

"In case what?"

"In case I was followed. Is that silly?"

"By no means. I'll drive you home."

"I can drive home all right, but if you could follow me in your car—"

"Sure."

* * * *

Heading for the office, I asked her a few more questions about what her mysterious visitors had looked like. She didn't have much to say about them.

"How about the lady from the assessor's office?" I asked her.

"She looked like somebody's mother, you know?"

"Sweet?"

"Very sweet, with bright, blue eyes."

"Gray hairs?"

"Blond. Ordinary blond."

"And the two who wanted to check for repairs?"

"Well, you saw the picture of Whisky Davis. The other one was a lot younger, and well built, like an athlete."

I pulled into my street, made a U-turn like a carom off the corner of Tony's joint across from the office, and slid into the white loading zone which is nearly always open after dark.

"So that's how you do it," Virgie said. "I went around the block twice. I was sure I'd get a ticket if I parked in the loading zone."

"You might have at that," I said. "I get quite a few, but it's cheaper than a garage."

We stopped in the office and I offered her a liqueur, which she declined. She sat comfortably in the chair, smoking her cigarette. Her white hands were unbelievably fragile-looking but perfectly formed. She had probably changed very little from the delicate, doll-like creature Henley had fallen for—as who wouldn't. I hoped the next guy would be a good one and would live a long time.

"I'll drive behind you on the way home," I said. "Do you have a garage?"

"No. I park on the street."

"I'll watch where you park and if I can't get in right behind you, please stay in your car till I've parked and come back. I'll go in with you and look around."

She stamped out her cigarette and got to her feet, light and quick.

"It's more than all right, it's wonderful," she said.

She smiled up at me sheepishly.

"I don't mind saying it now," she said. "I was getting scared. I mean real scared."

"I'll stay if you like—you must have a couch, something in the living room—"

"I have, but I'm sure I'll be all right once we've gotten home and you've checked the apartment."

"Then all right. You're a brave girl, and a lovely one, if I may say so."

"You may say so."

I switched off the lamp and followed her outside.

* * * *

Her car was parked half a block down the street, near the alley that runs through to Chicago Avenue. The street was practically deserted and our footsteps echoed in the quiet night. Virgie walked in a businesslike way, her purse slapping rhythmically against her thigh.

She found her keys and opened the door on the curb side of the car. I held it while she slid across the seat and under the wheel, then closed it quickly. She switched on the ignition and light came up. She leaned over to wave to me, smiling. I pointed to my car down the street and held up a hand, indicating I wanted her to wait a minute before pulling out. She nodded and settled under the wheel. She was reaching for the starter button as I backed off.

It was her last living moment. Virgie and the car blew up.

I remember screaming, but it was far, far too late. I was between two walls and they were pressing the wind out of me. Then suddenly they sprang apart and the air rushed back in. Then one of them fell on me and after that I felt nothing, nothing at all.

CHAPTER FOUR

It was hot in the room. The bed was hospital type and I was on it, naked to the waist, shoeless. I felt giddy, as if from dope, and bruised. There was a soft bandage just off my left eye so I couldn't see anything in that direction without turning my head.

The big guy hanging around the bed turned out to be Donovan, lieutenant type. His battered face resembled that of a pre-Colombian figurine. The only sign of impatience about him was the alternate tightening and relaxing of his mouth.

"Where is this meeting taking place?" I asked.

My voice sounded strange. He told me the name of a hospital and I started off the bed. He pushed me back.

"I can't afford it," I said. "At ten dollars a minute—"

"Take it easy," he rumbled. "It was handy. You can work out some arrangements."

"What happened?" I said.

"Suppose you tell me."

I forced myself to remember. It was like trying to put a heavy, awkward bundle on a high shelf too small to hold it, while standing on tiptoe in an off-balance position. I would get it up there and shove it back as far as possible; then I would start to relax and it would slip off.

"Do I have to?" I said.

"Well, I ain't got too much time."

I tried again.

"Virgie Henley," I said.

Donovan's face squeezed tight, then opened as he made the identification.

"The private eye that took the long dive a year ago?"

"His widow. You didn't know that yet? What time is it?"

"About three a.m. They might have made her downtown, there was an intact license plate."

The thing slipped off the shelf again and I let it fall.

"It's all down there now," Donovan said, like talking to himself. "Scraped it all up for the lab. You want to know somethin', I'm glad I'm not in that department."

It was his way of keeping me conversational. I took in some more of the room and decided not to worry too much about the bill. It was obviously a makeshift, spare-bedroom type of accommodation. Odds and ends of equipment were stored in corners. The walls were rough finished. There were doors that appeared to open on closets or storerooms. There was noise, clanking and banging, as if we were in the basement or a service area. A nurse came in, opened one of the doors, took out a couple of bedpans and left the room without looking at me. I felt better. I started to tell Donovan about Virgie Henley's last days.

It took quite a while because I kept getting mixed up and would have to go back and make corrections. Donovan was patient. We were about two thirds of the way through it when another nurse came in. She was a slip of a girl in red hair and freckles, and she came over to the bed and looked at me with a kind of pout and then grinned, and I tried to grin back, but it didn't work right so she stopped grinning right away.

"How do you feel?" she asked.

"Fine," I said. "Great. Don't give me any medicine without checking with my accountant."

"Do you want us to call your doctor?"

"Ah—no, thanks; I'll go to him this time. We sort of take turns."

"All right," she said.

She was cute. She made me think of Virgie, though they were really quite different—especially in the fact that the nurse was alive. She went over to one of the closets and puttered around and I went on reporting to Donovan. When I finished, he stood around chewing on it and the nurse went on puttering and I lay there and gradually got my curiosity back.

"How come I didn't blow up too?" I said.

"Dumb luck," Donovan said. "You blew clear—just hard enough to land on your neighbor's front steps, not quite hard enough to break your back."

"Which neighbor was it?" I said.

"I don't know."

"It was me, for one," the little nurse said unexpectedly. "I live in that building."

I looked at her.

"Right on a public street like that," I said, "they could rig her car?"

"Sure," Donovan said. "Takes about five minutes. You throw a jumper wire on the ignition and lead off to the cap—"

"All right, in a garage, out in the suburbs, but—"

"Come on, friend. When a small truck drives up beside a car and a guy in a mechanic's suit with a handful of tools throws up the hood, do you ask for his ID card? Unless it's your own car, naturally."

"But people see him, witnesses—"

"No," Donovan said tiredly. "Nobody sees. Nobody's ever watching."

"That's the way it was done then?"

"It could be. One convenient feature is that when it blows, it usually blows the traces too—fingerprints and the tracks and like that. So you depend on eyewitnesses which, as I just said, there ain't any and especially tonight, except you of course."

"Yeah."

He got out a notebook and a stub of pencil.

"What was this girl's address?"

I looked around for my coat.

"I wrote it down."

Donovan picked my coat off a chair and handed it to me. I went through some pockets and found the paper on which I had written Virgie's address. I read it off and Donovan wrote it down.

"You didn't write down any description of these mysterious people she mentioned?"

"No. Of course there's the one she identified for Sergeant Monday—Brophy's guy, Whisky Davis. But none of the others."

I told him what she had told me about them as nearly as I could remember. He made a few notes.

"How do you come to be doing this routine leg-work?" I asked him.

"I had a couple of boys here for a while, but I had to send them out. When I stopped by, they said you were comin' out of it."

My head hurt. He looked at his notes, scowling, stuck them in his pocket and took off his hat to scratch his head.

"Got the marks of some kind of Irish vendetta," he grumbled. "I got to go now. Keep in touch, huh?"

"Believe you me," I said. "Because it's a personal matter now. Not only was she a client, she was a great young lady, lonesome and scared, but great. You could put her in your pocket and site would always keep you warm. She was the original living doll."

He shrugged, worked at his hat and opened the door.

"If you say so," he said. "You couldn't tell any more, you know—after? So long, Dick Tracy."

"So long, cop."

* * * *

I sat up on the bed and stared at the redheaded nurse until she replaced the image of Virgie Henley. She finished something and glanced at me and jumped a little, startled.

"You'd better rest a little longer," she said.

"I better get going."

"How do you feel?" she said.

"We went through that before."

"I know. I'm supposed to keep track."

I slid carefully over the edge and got my feet on the floor and stood on them. I was very dizzy. I shook my head and it cleared some. I saw my shirt hanging on the chair where my coat had been. I took a couple of steps and it worked all right, so I walked over there for my shirt. The nurse came quickly and put her hand on the small of my back. It was shocking. Her hand was ridiculously small but warm and living. I shivered.

"You sure you want to get up now?" she said.

"No, but I might as well."

"Here, let me help you."

She held the shirt for me and I got into it and buttoned it. My fingers were clumsy and too big. She helped me with the buttons.

"Thanks," I said, "but I can stick it in my pants by myself."

She blushed and I was sorry.

"Excuse me," I said. "I mean you're a good girl to help me."

"There's medication left here," she said, "if you want it. You'll have to pay for it anyway."

I put the little cellophane package in my pocket.

"Can I get you anything else?" she asked.

"How about a cup of coffee?"

She looked disturbed.

"The coffee shop is closed—"

"Well, forget it; thanks anyway."

I sat down on a chair and groped for my shoes with the socks stuffed in them.

"Just like home," I said.

She was standing there, watching me.

"You wait a minute," she said, "I'll be right back."

"It's all right," I said, "I won't try to jump my bill."

"Oh, no! I didn't mean that. You wait here."

"Yes, ma'am."

I put on my shoes and socks and hung my tie around my neck, leaving my collar open, got into my coat and checked around to see that I had everything I ought to have. My hat was hanging on a hook beside the door. I took it down and was getting it into shape when the nurse came back. She was carrying two paper cups of coffee.

"Angel of mercy!" I said.

"From the nurses' lounge," she said. "It's against the rules, but—" She pushed the door to with her foot. I relieved her of one of the cups. It smelled delicious. It was hotter than thirty pistols so I couldn't tell much about the taste. We stood around drinking it.

"I heard you telling the officer—" she said.

"That was Donovan," I said. "Not just 'the officer.' Anybody can be an officer. That was Donovan."

"Oh—" she looked startled. "I'm sorry. I heard you telling him about that poor girl. I'm sorry—was she your girl?"

"No. I don't have a girl right now."

"I heard the explosion," she said, "way over here inside the hospital. We didn't know what it was till the policeman brought you in here."

I drank the coffee and looked at her. She was awfully good to look at, but it embarrassed her and I quit it. I took a card from my pocket.

"If I can be of any assistance to you at any time," I said.

"Oh, thanks," she said, blushing, "but I don't need a card."

"Got a perfect memory?"

"No—you're Mac. I know about you."

"I see."

"I've seen you around—Tony's and places."

"You girls hang around Tony's?" I said. "Is that permitted?"

She laughed and blushed some more. When she blushed she looked very pink.

I emptied my cup, crumpled it and threw it into a large tin receptacle near the door. The nurse stopped laughing and looked very serious. She put her hand on my arm and I could feel it warm through my jacket.

"Are you sure you're all right?"

I patted her in a fatherly way.

"I'll be fine, honey. Thanks for the coffee. Where do I take care of the bill?"

"When you go out there by the big receiving entrance, there's a desk. They'll take care of it."

"I'll bet they will."

"It won't be too bad, don't worry."

I gave her the victory sign and she responded hesitantly. I went out and found the desk and the bill came to about twenty-eight dollars, which wasn't bad at all, considering.

It was only a couple of blocks from the hospital to my place, so I walked. It was cold and the wind had risen again. I stayed on the opposite side of the street from my office and where the nurse lived farther down the block. There was a cluster of people still hanging around the place where it had happened; a growling undertone of babble. A couple of them were prowling the street, looking for souvenirs. One of them even had a flashlight.

CHAPTER FIVE

The walk from the hospital was bracing. I poured a little brandy in a big glass and inhaled it for a while. I was wide awake and I knew it wouldn't do any good to go to bed without taking something and I didn't know what they had given me at the hospital. Besides, I would have been afraid to go to sleep. The only way I could keep down the horror of what had happened to Virgie was to stay on edge. I sat with the brandy and kept track of the time and in this way passed about an hour and a half. At five-fifteen a.m. I dialed the residence telephone number of Paul Budge, Attorney at Law.

The phone rang three times, there was a click and it rang some more, differently. Answering service. Finally a woman answered. I gave her my name and said I needed urgently to speak to Mr. Budge. She said Mr. Budge wasn't in his office yet. I said I knew that but would she please wake him up for me because it was very urgent. She said she couldn't do that. I said that if she didn't do it for me now she would have to do it for the police pretty soon because it had to do with the murder of one of Mr. Budge's clients.

"One moment, sir," she said.

I hung on for a minute and a sleepy man's voice said, "Yes, what is it?"

I told him who I was. It took some time to get through to his brain.

"Oh, yes," he said finally. "I know. Go ahead."

I told him Virgie Henley had been murdered.

"What—no! Look, don't play games—"

"No game, Mr. Budge. I saw it happen."

"This is on the level?"

"Squarely."

"I can't—"

"Yes. Well, I think we ought to have a talk as soon as possible. Virgie came to see me about some things."

He was waking up rather nicely.

"Of course," he said. "I'll meet you—I guess my office would be most convenient for both of us." He gave me the address in the Loop. "Take me about forty-five minutes," he said.

I told him I would be there.

* * * *

At about ten minutes to six I was walking up and down in front of the LaSalle Street building where Budge kept an office. It was a gray hour, light enough to show up the dirt and clutter of the Loop without any compensation of sunshine or the sound of commerce. The grinding rumble of early morning trucks was a different sound, hard and hostile.

At one minute after six, a taxi pulled in and a man I took to be Budge got out of it. He was middle-aged, in a tweed coat over a blue suit, and he carried a slim brief case. He had the well-tended, somewhat puffy but disciplined face of the professional city man who makes an adequate living with not much left over for Miami or Las Vegas.

We shook hands.

"Pleasure to meet you," he said hurriedly while he unlocked the street door of the building. "Great shock to me naturally—come on in."

We got through the door awkwardly but safely and into an elevator and eventually made his modest suite on the tenth floor. On the door was the name, Paul Budge, Attorney; and farther down in smaller letters, Eric P. Safford.

I followed him through a reception room into a private office with three windows, and two doors in opposite walls. One was open, and beyond it I could see a small library with stacks of books from floor to ceiling. Budge set about opening blinds and windows.

"Make yourself comfortable," he said.

"Who is Safford?" I asked. "Partner?"

"Not exactly. Sort of associate, young fellow. He helps me and I try to help him."

He got into a chair behind his desk, switched on the desk lamp, leaned forward in a businesslike way and nodded.

"Tell me about it," he said.

I started at the beginning, with Virgie's visit to me. I gave him the whole thing, including as much of our conversation as I could recall. When I got to the windup, the quick, total disaster, he put his hand over his eyes and shook his head as if in pain.

"It's unbelievable," he said.

"I know," I said. "But I believe it."

He sat with it for a minute. I looked at my watch and wondered what time the storage company would be open for business.

"What did you tell Lieutenant Donovan?"

"Everything I've told you," I said, "except that I didn't mention you—mainly because I didn't think of it."

"Well—" he was uneasy in his chair. "I mean, what did you want of me?"

"I'd like to go through Barry Henley's files."

"Oh."

"And the sooner we can get to it, the better, because Donovan and the department will be around shortly."

"Yes." He ran his tongue over his lips. "It's risky. I don't like to fool around with it."

"Not too risky," I said. "You haven't had any word from the police. Nobody official has been asking for the files. Technically you don't know anything about it, except that something happened to Virgie. Therefore you have a right to break those seals."

"I know, but technical is only technical. I actually know more than that. I can reasonably expect an order to produce the files at any moment, and if they turn up with the seals broken, the police may not like it."

"I have no intention of making away with anything," I said. "I just want to look through those files before they get away from us, to try to put a few things together. I had hoped we could do this together—sort of a mutual watchdog operation."

He gazed at me. I couldn't read him and I was getting edgy. One telephone call and we could be cooked. It was true I didn't mean to withhold anything from the cops. I didn't even want to get a jump on them. But I knew that once the files were in police hands I might never get a look at them.

"I'm afraid I don't get your urgency," Budge said. "I don't mean to be crude, but your client is dead. There's really nothing you have to do about the case—if you're thinking of a fee from the estate—"

I got up.

"The hell with that," I said. "I have the most basic reason in the world. Whoever blew up Virgie and her car had to know she had come to see me. He—or they—don't know what she may have told me. He might logically expect me to be in possession of whatever he's been wanting, or at least to have information about it, whatever it is. And we know this, that whatever it is, he wants it badly. I don't want to get blown to bits, Mr. Budge. I bet you don't either."

He made a couple of passes with his hands. His face frowned. I knew I had lost this round, and time was flying.

"Nevertheless," he said, "you understand my position—"

"All right," I said, backing to the door. "I'll take my chances with the police."

I opened the door and got into the corridor. I went fast to the elevator. Downstairs in the big, marble lobby I found the rear exit directly in line with the front entrance, though screened by an elaborate planter. Across from the elevator bank was an alcove, partially closed by a standing screen. I went back there and found a crack.

Three minutes dragged by. The building watchman came clanking along the corridor from the rear, passed the alcove and the elevators and paused in the middle of the lobby to check his timepiece. With a last look around he went to the front door and unlocked it, then clanked off to the side of the lobby and disappeared.

I could hear one of the elevators working. It hissed, thudded gently and came to a stop. Paul Budge got out of it and crossed the lobby briskly. He was dressed for the street and was carrying his brief case. I left the alcove, got to the door and stayed out of sight until he had flagged his taxi. Things were going my way and another cab had drawn in to replace the first. I made it before the driver could kill his motor.

"Follow, huh?" I said.

"Sure, Jack."

* * * *

We went around the block and headed west, beyond the Loop, out past the Daily News plaza. Gradually, block by block, the early morning traffic thickened. In another hour the streets would be teeming with the shock troops of the business army—the little expendable people. The higher echelons would follow at a more leisurely pace.

Budge's cab drove up at the front entrance of the city's most prominent moving and storage company, a massive concrete and steel structure whose uppermost facade was just now catching the first glint of morning sunlight. It was shortly after seven o'clock and I was surprised that the place would be open to anyone. Then I remembered that the advertised keynote of the firm was "24-hour service." You could move by this outfit's facilities from Chicago to anywhere in the United States or Canada and all you had to do for yourself was to pack a few personal necessities, book your passage and relax. When you were ready to move into your new home, you would find everything in place and a fire laid. For a slight extra fee, they would arrange to cater your first meal and do the dishes after.

I caught up with Budge at the big glass doors of the entrance. He was startled but controlled himself well. His mouth twisted in a half smile.

"I should have known better," he said.

"I figure I've earned a look at those files. And I didn't try to con you, did I? I might have."

"You might," he said grimly. "Since you're here you might as well come along."

"Thanks," I said.

At a reception desk Budge showed credentials and signed something. We were transported downstairs by an automatic elevator. There was a comfortable reception room and lounge. It was unattended, but I had the feeling it wouldn't take long for someone to show in a crisis. It was quiet. The vaults and cold storage facilities were camouflaged by a tasteful decor and a screen partially blocking a concrete corridor.

Budge lit a cigarette and smoked it assiduously. There was a rumble of voices. It turned into the rumble of steel wheels on concrete. A man in the storage company uniform trundled in a metal file cabinet on a dolly. Behind him in khaki, wearing a badge and gun, came a private officer with a clipboard.

They set the cabinet up for us and Budge identified himself for the officer and signed something on the clipboard, after checking to make sure the seals were still intact. Then the two of them went away and there we were with Barry Henley's files.

The rest was anticlimactic. Budge dug out a key and stuck it in the lock at the top of the cabinet, then hesitated, turning to me.

"What did you have in mind?" he asked.

"You know my objective as well as I do," I said. "I want to know what Barry was working on at the time of his death—and anything that might be pertinent to it."

He nodded, frowning. I tried to reassure him.

"If you know of something in there that is highly confidential and that you know for sure has no connection with Henley's or Virgie's deaths, and if you give me your solemn word on it, I might be inclined to accept it. But I don't see how that would be possible because Virgie told me you had never been through these files yourself."

"That's true," he said.

I was on ice so thin my feet were wet. I had no license to examine those files and Budge would be well within his rights to tell me to go to hell. But he had already shown that he wanted to get into them himself and I could figure that he would avoid a showdown.

He wasn't a soft touch though.

"This is close to coercion," he said. "You realize that?"

"I'm not going to threaten or use force. It's up to you."

I had him. Force, threats, he could have dealt with. He could have turned me over to the officer with the gun who, though out of sight, was probably within hailing distance. But the implied moral argument was stronger. We were in this together and eventually he faced it. He twisted the key in the lock and it snapped open. He took a penknife out of his pocket and slit the paper seal at the top of each drawer. Then he put the knife away, nodded brusquely and we were off.

A-B-C-D-E-

There were many folders and a lot of paper but the meat was pathetically lean. Barry Henley would have been hard put to make ends meet on the business that showed in the files. Of course he might have had side lines. I had my eye out for the side lines.

The alphabetical arrangement made it hard for me to construct a pattern of development in time. The dates were a jumble, as if they had been tossed in a hopper and spilled out at random. In the "B" file, we might find a collection item dated early 1957; a domestic relations job dated two years later; then a couple more collections and so on. There were more collection jobs than anything else. Industrial espionage is for the big organizations. Collection and skip tracing are the bread and butter of most of us free lancers. The trick is to get the big ones. Barry was starting from scratch and he had a lot of little ones, nickels and dimes. It would add up over a period of time, but it would keep your weight down and wear out your shoe leather in a hurry. If this is all you ever get to do, you scratch for it as long as your nails hold out, then wind up as somebody's night watchman, or maybe in a small hotel.

We were slowed down, too, by the necessity of watching each other closely to make sure neither of us slipped anything into a side pocket. Budge was sweating with the effort and there was some moisture on my own lip. I had a spread of time firm in my mind as the crucial period: between Christmas and Easter approximately one year previous. Barry had taken his long, fatal fall during the first week in March.

Budge and I were on either side of the drawer, fingering our way at the same pace, eying each other from time to time. It would have looked pretty funny to an outsider, but Budge was solemn and I was still reacting to Virgie's murder as I might have reacted to the bashing out of a baby's brains against a dirty wall. We were somewhere in the middle of the "E's" when I got fed up with the drag.

"This is no way," I said. "Let's take the damn drawers out. You take one, I'll take another. Then we'll switch."

He looked at me.

"Well—" he said.

I raised my right hand.

"Before we leave, you can search me; okay?"

"All right," he said.

"I get the same privilege?"

"What?"

"If you search me, I search you."

He nodded. It didn't mean a thing but it kept him off balance. I was getting a little upset with him and his obstructionism.

We lifted out the top drawer and then the second. I took the first and sat on the floor with it and Budge did the same with the second. I finished far ahead of him and went back for a quick double check. I didn't find anything within the allotted time span that I couldn't eliminate after a short study. I pushed the drawer within Budge's reach and took out the third one on my own. I opened the fourth, but it was empty. Apparently Barry had exhausted the alphabet in drawer number three: "S" to "Z."

I reached in at random and the break came. I pulled out a manila envelope exhibiting the typical, edge-curled profile of its contents. They had to be photographs. A little hunch crawled up my fingers and did a small dance in my head. I forced it to the back and opened the envelope. After a moment I glanced up to find Budge watching me intently.

There were six 8x10 portraits and about a dozen smaller ones of a woman of striking loveliness: a brunette, not older than Virgie Henley. Aside from this, they had little in common. This was obviously a big girl, probably statuesque. The shot was of the glamour type for publicity or fan mail purposes. She was partially reclining with one arm over her head. She wore a tender smile and a trick dress, designed to expose ample cleavage. She was not exceptionally blessed in that area, but it was a good, well-rounded view. Her face had been carefully arranged to avoid a leer, so the face came out sweet and wholesome American-girlish. The total effect was of something that could be tacked on the wall of a prep school dormitory and left there, even during Mother's visit. On the back of one of the 8x10s was a stamped date: January 16, 1958.

Budge didn't quite contain himself.

"Pictures?" he asked casually.

"Uh-Huh. Nice pictures."

I had to have one of them, and the longer I delayed getting one into my pocket, the poorer would be my chances.

Taking the chance that Budge had noticed only the 8x10s, I slid them out of the envelope slowly, thumbing off and then palming one of the smaller copies in the process. He was so intent on the big pictures I handed him that he lost track of my other hand. I got the smaller copy in my coat pocket, dropped the envelope back in the file and started looking on both sides of it for whatever it connected with.

It didn't take long. This had been Barry's "big one." The folder was thin, but the dates of the material—hurried notations on scraps of paper, a few pages of typescript, some faded newspaper clippings—showed that he had been on the case from January 16 to March 3.

"What was the date of Barry's death?" I asked.

"March fourth," Budge said, looking up from the pictures.

I had a pencil in my hand and was making notes rapidly.

"Who's the girl in the picture?" I asked.

"I don't know."

"Does the name Stanhope mean anything to you?"

"No," he said.

Stanhope was the name on the index tab of the file folder. My accumulating notes read as follows:

"Stanhope, Riverwood; morning Jan. 16: Carolyn S., 22, brun., 5-5, sng. &: dance, last book Hi Hat, Xmas to N. Y.; last message Xmas cd. from No. Side address Dec. 15."

I had gleaned this from fuller but nearly illegible notes in what must have been Barry's hand, probably jotted down at the time he received the assignment. On one of the typed pages was a partial progress report from Jan. 16 to Feb. 1. It was pitifully scanty. Henley had traced back through the Hi Hat Club booking, the North Side street address; had found an agent who had handled the girl during the previous summer and had no idea of her present whereabouts; had checked out half a dozen other people and had come up with nothing. I passed that much over to Budge and went on. There was a gap of several weeks. Around February 15, Henley had made a few notes on another scrap of paper:

"Carolyn contacted Lundquist (this girl hooked? ask old man?)." This was the first indication that the girl's father was the client—if he was her father. The "old man" might be anyone. "Lundquist claims no knowledge whereabouts." It wasn't clear whether Lundquist was male or female, or owned a telephone or an address.

There were some miscellaneous entries between Feb. 15 and 25. Then a newspaper clipping dated Feb. 28. It was a two-inch story under a one-line head:

LATE DEB HOME FROM EAST:—Miss Dorothy Stanhope, whose coming-out a few seasons back was the affair of the year, has cut short her Eastern trip in order to be at the bedside of her father (that's the steel Stanhope, kids) who has been ill for several weeks. Miss Stanhope said she plans to remain in Riverwood until family plans shall have jelled.

I read it again, carefully, with variations. Although the carefully edited society note was pregnant with hints, especially the last lovely phrase, "when family plans shall have jelled" (for which read: "when family problems can be straightened out—such as what happened to poor Carolyn and how much longer does the old man have to live?"), it didn't tell me anything more useful than that there was a Stanhope girl named Dorothy whose father was sick. I didn't know whether Carolyn S. was a Stanhope, or, if so, whether she was sister, cousin, aunt or niece.

The last item in the folder was an empty envelope (originally designed to transmit a gas bill) on which Barry Henley had scrawled a few hurried notes under date of March 3. Some were illegible. I made it as follows, complete with blanks:

> Stanhope place 3:00 p.m. urg. lady—(illegible)—& witn. Stanhope clear in head; good guy, too bad.
> Bill to date—D. Stanhope calling off hunt. Why?
> Expenses Mar. 3, nil; profit ditto.

There was no duplicate invoice in the file. I wondered how much Barry had made on the case over that six-week stretch. Judging from the notes, he had not located Carolyn S(tanhope?) and the family, or at least Dorothy Stanhope, ex-debutante and bedside vigilante, had decided to call off the search. One day later, Barry had died. Was there a connection? No evidence. But there was nothing else in the files that could have any more of a connection, so it looked as if the Stanhope affair was what we were stuck with.

"Does this case ring any bell with you?" I asked Budge.

He looked up and regarded me fishily. I was getting claustrophobia in the vault and he made me nervous.

"Stanhope," I said. "The Stanhope case."

"Oh—no, the name means nothing to me."

"Barry never mentioned it?"

"No."

He put the folder in the file and got up and took a turn around the room.

"I don't know what preconceptions you have," he said, "but you must realize I didn't know Barry well. I knew his wife even less. I got involved with these files because he came to see me a few times and in a sort of off-hand, tenuous way, he became a client."

I got up, shrugged into my jacket and reset my hat.

"What did he consult you about?" I asked.

"Small things—tax matters, legal points involved in his cases."

"All right. Let's blow this crummy vault."

"I'm not quite finished," he said.

"Whatever you say. Help you stick those drawers back in?"

"I'll manage, thanks. Are you planning to follow up the Stanhope line?"

"I guess so. It's what we've got."

"I'd appreciate it if you'd keep in touch with me."

I let some time pass.

"Well," I said, "maybe. If you have a strong interest in this, maybe we can come to an understanding."

"I'm not offering to retain you."

"Oh. I'm disappointed."

"It's just that if I can help you in any way that won't violate a confidence—"

I held my peace and he got edgy.

"As you can see," he said, "it was a rather light reed on which to hang a relationship, but I did a few chores for them and I guess Virgie naturally turned to me when Barry died."

"Sure," I said.

I offered again to help him replace the file drawers, but he declined and I straightened my hat again and left. When I got back to my office, Donovan was sitting in his car at the curb, waiting.

CHAPTER SIX

I invited him in for a cup of coffee but he shook his head.

"No time," he said. "Where you been?"

"Here and there," I said. "What's new?"

I climbed into the car and sat down with him in the back seat.

"Did you check out Virgie Henley's apartment?" I asked him.

"Uh-huh. Somebody beat us to it."

"Oh?"

"Big search. Place was a shambles. Cut to ribbons."

"Then they must have gone over it right after they wired the car."

"What happened to Henley's files?" Donovan asked.

"Virgie told me a lawyer named Paul Budge had helped her get them ready for storage."

"In storage? Sealed?"

"Yeah."

Donovan sighed.

"Then we got to go to the Supreme Court, huh?"

"Maybe not. You can probably deal with Budge. Homicide, involved, no client to protect any more."

"You sound as if you know."

I shrugged. Donovan didn't press it. It was one of those inexplicable breaks you get.

"What do you think?" he asked.

"I don't know," I said. "It's a drastic step to kill someone just in order to get a look at her apartment. There has to be more motive."

We sat there.

"I ran across something," I said. "I can't say where—might have a connection. Does the name Stanhope mean anything to you?"

"Police-wise?" he said.

"Maybe."

I don't know whether he racked his brain or not, but he seemed to give it some thought. Finally he said, "There was a very well-off guy named Stanhope lived out west, Riverwood somewhere. Guy in the steel business."

"That's the one."

I showed him the picture of Carolyn S.

"So what?" he said.

I told him what I had surmised from the notes in Barry's file. I didn't mention the file itself. When I finished, he looked doubtful, as he should have.

"That's a long time ago," he said. "You could go to a lot of trouble trying to connect that with the explosion and come up with nothing at all."

"You could," I agreed. "But what else have we got?"

He looked at me out of his bruised face.

"All right," I said, "you already told me you're too busy to have a cup of coffee. What are you hanging around gassing with me for? All I know I already told you."

"Don't get uppity," he said. "You may have a private interest in this that wouldn't make any difference to me."

"I have," I said, "and maybe it doesn't make any difference to you. You have to look into it because you get paid for it. I'm looking into it because I've got a personal beef with whoever blew up Virgie and her car. I've got enough cushion in my bank account to take time for it. We can work together or we can race each other in blindfolds."

I climbed out of the car. Donovan mumbled something and his driver got the motor going.

"All right," he said, "I'll work with you."

"It's a deal." I closed the door and leaned in through the open window. "So what have you got?"

"Nothin'," he said. "Nothin' at all."

"Then I'll keep in touch," I said.

"Okay."

The car pulled away and I watched it out of sight. I turned up the street toward the scene of the explosion, but after a few paces I stopped and went back the other way. There were two or three people hanging around there and I couldn't stand the thought of it. I was afraid one of them might come up with a fragment of delicate, blue-veined, blood-pinked human tissue and ask me to confirm its authenticity.

I went into the office, picked up the early mail and checked with my answering service. There was nothing that couldn't wait. Outside on the steps of the building I looked down at my car, parked at the curb.

No, I thought, they wouldn't rig my car too. They would figure I had useful information and I wouldn't be any good to them dead.

But they rigged Virgie's car, didn't they? And she's dead.

But maybe they figured they would get me with the same charge, so they didn't bother to fix mine too.

Only why would they want to get me?

Why would they want to get Virgie?

They were good solid questions looking for an answer. I could think of no way to find the answer while standing on my own steps, admiring my overpriced, under-engineered automobile.

I went down there and took a turn around the car. It looked no different from the way it had looked eighteen hours earlier, before Virgie died. I stood back at arm's length and opened the left door carefully.

Nothing happened. I leaned in and released the hood latch, ducking back when the hinges sprang. I eased the door to, walked up front and raised the hood.

It took a while, with my limited mechanical knowledge, to check the places I could think of. When I finished I hadn't found anything unusual, but I wasn't sure I had covered every possibility.

I gave the hood a brisk push and jumped back about six feet. Nothing exploded. But that didn't prove much either.

I walked around it again, stalling, and I was having those prickly heat sensations in the back of my neck and around my eyes, imagining everyone watching me from concealment—behind curtains at every window on the block.

But a man would be foolish to climb under the wheel, hit the starter button and blow himself to hell in order to put up a front for the neighbors.

The auto club!

It was a brilliant flash, except that I couldn't think of a way to set forth my predicament without some loss of face.

I looked over my left shoulder, then my right, walked around the car once more, pretending to check the tires, and wound up again at the door. I opened it firmly enough and slid onto the seat and all was normal. I slammed the door shut and held on tight and nothing out of the way happened. I fooled around with the gadgets, rolled the window up, then rolled it down again and drew in some fresh air. It inflated my chest jerkily. The starter button was a huge eye looking back at me. I caressed it without love. It was only a small protuberance of steel, cold and smooth and uncompromising. I set my thumb against it, hooked my fingers under the rim of the dash, took hold of the window ledge with my other hand and counted to ten. I pushed the button.

All that happened was that the car rumbled to life. It was a little cold and it spat a few times, but it kept going. Nothing blew up.

I leaned back, loosened my collar, wiped my face with my handkerchief and let the motor warm up at leisure. Gradually the objects, moving and stationary, that I could see through the windshield swam into a sort of focus. I could feel sweat running down from my armpits and down the middle of my back. My right hand was shaking a little. Funny thing. My left hand was all right. Only my right was shaking. I checked on this and found that my left hand was still gripping the window ledge. My knuckles were chalk-white. I forced the hand to relax.

A powerful black sedan whooshed up from behind and the tires squawked a little, stopping. The back door opened and Donovan leaned out.

"Forgot to tell you," he said, "I had the bomb detail go over your car, just in case. It was clean as a whistle."

I got out my handkerchief again, blew my nose, pushed back my hat and wiped my brow and flicked at a few imaginary flies. (They seemed real.)

"Thank you, my true friend," I said. "There's something I forgot to tell you, too."

"Yeah?"

"Yeah. I went through Barry Henley's files this morning."

He looked at me with a blank face. He got out a cigar and bit off the end and stuck it in his mouth, rolling it around some. Then he nodded.

"I figured," he said. "So long, Scotty."

"Erin go bragh," I said.

He pulled away with something of a flourish and I had myself a spit out the window and put the thing in gear. With the disciplining over and done with, maybe now we could get on with the job.

CHAPTER SEVEN

Behind a chest-high counter on the main floor of the B and D Hotel and Restaurant Supply Co was a woman of indeterminate age, wearing a severe look and a pince-nez on a black ribbon. Beyond her in a glass cubicle, a fluffy-looking blonde with round shoulders sat hunched over a typing desk.

"Mr. Brophy in?" I asked.

She gave me an extremely severe look.

"Can anyone else help you?" she asked.

There were a couple of fellows wandering around the barnlike room, picking their way among light fixtures, decorative screens, upholstery samples, china and glassware. They looked like salesmen.

"I don't know," I said. "How about Whisky Davis?"

She gave me the severity on a Whisky Davis level.

"I was referred to him, or Mr. Brophy," I said. "I'm planning to open a joint—I mean a small club and this friend said Mr. Brophy was the man to see. But if I couldn't see Brophy, I should settle for Davis."

She looked at me both severely and impatiently and picked up a telephone at her left hand. I heard a buzzing and a lady's voice on the other end.

"A gentleman to see Mr. Davis," she said. "It's about some equipment. He was referred to Mr. Davis personally—"

She covered the mouthpiece and gave me another look.

"Whom did you say referred you?" she asked.

I glanced around and gave it to her with the corner of my mouth, low and mumbly.

"Pete Ruga," I said.

She looked sort of puzzled, then said it into the mouthpiece loud and clear. It sounded different when she said it, like a different name, more authentic.

She hung up, pulled a pencil from behind her ear and pointed across the floor with it.

"Take the elevator to the ninth floor," she said. "The receptionist will show you where to go."

"Thank you, ma'am," I said.

She looked disgusted and went back to the cubicle where the blonde was pecking at the typewriter.

I walked kind of tight past the two salesmen on the floor, giving them no notice. The main trick in playing tough guy is not to give anybody any notice. It didn't seem to bother them.

Up on the ninth floor, it didn't bother the deep-bosomed, Titian-haired lovely with the ornate glasses and pointed chin; but then, I did give her a certain amount of notice.

"Sit down, please," she said in a monotone. "Mr. Davis will be right out."

Her blue eyes behind the glasses were abnormally large. I decided she was either exceptionally nearsighted or had incipient goiter. Which would be a shame.

I sat down on a gold brocade settee and waited. There weren't any magazines to look at and the receptionist sat virtually motionless, so about all I had to do was to sit there and look at my thumbs.

The room wasn't unpleasant. The lights were subdued, the furnishings tasteful, the ventilation adequate, even without windows. If you were planning to open a restaurant or hotel, I thought, you could hardly find a nicer place in which to arrange for your equipment.

Still something was wrong, something beyond the pervasive background knowledge that dealing with Brophy was likely to be not only disadvantageous but painful. I couldn't put my finger on it and tried to discount it as a projection of my own mood, but I couldn't shake the bad feeling. In an effort to shake it, I concentrated on trying to deduce the layout of this ninth floor in relation to what I had seen from across the alley. But it's hard to get oriented in a sealed room.

The girl with the big eyes made a move. What she did, she sat up straighter in her chair. It made her about an inch taller. Somehow I reasoned that we could expect Mr. Davis any moment. How she knew, I couldn't figure out; there were no flashing lights, no buzzings, nothing I could see or hear. Maybe it was something you felt when you had been around long enough. Anyway, my hunch proved out. A door opened behind the girl's chair and a guy came into the room.

It was the mug Virgie had identified: a long face with a good chin, wide-set and somewhat puckered eyes with generous gray pouches underneath; a slight scar, a thin mouth and brilliant, even, strong-looking teeth.

Before a word could be spoken, the receptionist got up, smoothed her skirt down her hips, picked up a package of cigarettes and left the room, walking tight and controlled. I watched her, wondering whether she was the girl I had seen the day before through the window. It sent me into a fit of depression, thinking how rough this job was going to be if I would have to go around snatching wigs in order to identify ladies' heads.

For quite a long time, Davis and I did nothing but look at each other. He was better at it than I, maybe because I had too much interest in him. Finally he said something and I caught the significance of the moniker, Whisky. His voice was thin and hoarse and every so often it would break into another register, like a boy's voice changing. I dug his message only with difficulty. He said something with a question mark that sounded like it might have been the name I had dropped downstairs.

"Pete Ruga?"

I didn't know whether there was any such person as Pete Ruga, so I said, "Yeah."

"Where ya plan t'openna joint?" I think he said.

"Cicero," I said, picking a likely spot.

"Unh," he said.

So there we were.

"So whaddya want I mean?" he said.

I spread my hands to show we understood each other.

"Mr. Brophy here?" I asked.

He thought about that. He thought about it so long I cracked under the strain.

"Haven't you got some kind of private office?" I asked.

"Go ahead," Davis said. "This is private. So whaddya want I mean?"

This could go on forever, I thought. I didn't want to squeeze things to a head before I knew where Brophy was. Preferably I wanted Brophy in on the conversation.

"I been planning this joint a while," I said. "Coupla years. I remember Henley telling me, when I got ready, you know, I should drop in and see Brophy."

"Who?" Davis said.

"Brophy."

"No, I mean before."

"Oh—Henley. Barry Henley. Some kind of private eye, you know? He got knocked off one night about a year ago."

Davis didn't say whether he knew about that or not. He scratched the back of his neck and straightened his tie some and looked at me and I wondered where Brophy was.

Sometimes you don't begin to make progress until after you've given up.

"Maybe I picked the wrong day," I said, getting on my feet. "I got time—shop around a while—"

I headed for the door by which I had entered.

"Hold it," Davis said. "Come in the office."

I turned and he was showing me which way to go behind the reception-ist's desk. I went. He pushed the door open and I walked past him into a large office. Nothing small-time about Brophy.

I gathered it was Brophy at the big desk; a stringy guy with leathery skin and a tight mouth that didn't move much, even when he talked. Fifty maybe, maybe more or less, but watchful, wary, alert. He had gray hair cropped short, and toward the back of his skull it was getting thin.

There was another guy in the room but I hardly noticed him. He was standing off to one side. The glance I gave him told me only that he was much younger than either Davis or Brophy and that he was built on the order of Max Baer, which was an efficient way to be built indeed.

Brophy didn't look at me. He looked at Davis.

"Who's he?" he said.

"He don't say," Davis told him.

It had been a mistake. I ought to have given a name.

"Who sent him?"

"Pete Ruga," Davis said, dead-pan.

Brophy looked at me. It scared the hell out of me.

"I never heard of a Pete Ruga," he said.

"Me neither," Davis said "What's he want?"

He was looking at me now but talking to Davis.

"Says he's gonna open a joint. Says Henley sent him."

"Who?"

"Henley. The one that died."

Brophy finally addressed me directly.

"What's your name?"

"What's the difference?" I asked. "You in business or what?"

I was aware that the young one with the big shoulders was moving. With Davis on one side and him on the other, not to mention Brophy dead ahead, there was only one way for me to go. Back. But Davis had moved too, and in the middle of my second step he kicked the legs out from under me. I went down hard, knocking my hat off and banging my head on the floor. It wasn't like taking the blast of the explosion that had killed Virgie, but it hurt more, possibly because of the loss of dignity.

It would have been ridiculous to fight back. The young one with the hands was going through my pockets. I left him alone. All he wanted was my wallet. He tossed it onto Brophy's desk, then gave me a hand up.

"Thanks," I said.

Brophy opened my wallet and studied it and threw it to me. It fell on the floor and I leaned over and picked it up.

"Another private eye," Brophy said. "What do you want?"

"I'll level with you," I said, "but let me clear up one point. I'm not just another private eye. I've got a mission."

"What?" he said.

"To find out who killed Virgie Henley."

"Who?"

"Mrs. Barry Henley. A widow, who died last night of an explosion in her car."

"Oh, that one," he said.

He drummed on his desk.

"A personal thing," he said.

"Intensely personal."

There were six telephones on his desk. He put his hand on one of them and pulled it within reach.

"You came to the wrong place," he said. "Blow."

"You have to start somewhere," I said.

"How come me?" he said.

"I'm not giving out that it makes a case," I said, "and it could be a mistake. But a few hours before she died, Mrs. Henley was looking at some mug shots—if you'll excuse the expression—and she came across one that seemed to belong to Mr. Davis."

It was quite still. I could hear Davis breathe.

"Mrs. Henley identified him—tentatively, you understand—as one of two men who had come to her apartment a few days ago and tried to gain admittance under a pretext. Inasmuch as Mrs. Henley had admitted previous mysterious callers of this nature, she got a little worried and came to see me. Unfortunately she died before she got a chance to confront Mr. Davis in the flesh."

Brophy picked the telephone off the hook and rubbed his nose with it. Nobody said anything.

"That was a long speech, I admit," I said, "but it's level. Maybe I could take a turn at asking questions."

Brophy nestled the phone thing against his neck and looked at me.

"Does the name Stanhope mean anything to you?" I asked.

He replaced the phone gently. He put his hands on the arms of his chair and slid it back. He got up and jerked his head at Davis and then he went through a door into the next room. He left the door open.

"Go ahead," Davis said hoarsely.

I followed Brophy. Davis and Mr. America followed me. I found Brophy in what had to be the room I had seen the day before, when I had noted the bald-headed lady. He was standing at the window through which I had seen her.

"Come over here," he said.

I moved somewhat closer with reluctance. He fingered the handles on the window frame and raised it, pretty high up. A cold draft swirled into the room.

"Come here," he said. "Show you something."

I moved close enough to look out and down a few stories; not all the way. I felt I could see quite well from where I stood.

Mr. America felt otherwise. Without warning, he had two handfuls of my coat and was hip-crowding me to the open window. I reached up in panic and grabbed the raised sash. He held me from behind, pushing me far enough out that I could have had an unobstructed view of the entire alley from end to end and side to side, if I had been looking. But my eyes were closed. Possibly I was praying, or trying to clear the cold, damp air out of my throat.

I could hear good though.

"Look down," Brophy said. "That private eye Henley died right down there. On the cement. I wasn't here. They told me about it the next morning. I said I was sorry."

The double grip on my coat tugged, then relaxed. I pushed back from the window and stood there, adjusting my coat and breathing.

"I run a business here," Brophy was saying. "Any time you want to buy any equipment, come on up. Any other time, stay the hell out."

He meant it all right and there wasn't much to be got out of him now. I turned around and walked away from him, past Davis and Mr. America into the big office. I found the door to the reception room and went out there. The large-breasted girl with the bug eyes was sitting at her desk reading a paperback novel. I looked closely at her hair as I passed, but I couldn't tell anything about it except that there was a lot of it and it was a pink-orange color. As nearly as I could tell, she didn't look at me at all.

I went down in the elevator and across the floor, and outside. I walked a few blocks to a saloon and bought a slug of whisky. In the men's room I washed my hands and face and put a clean band-aid on my cheekbone. Then I got in my car and headed west for Riverwood.

CHAPTER EIGHT

It was crisp and cold in Riverwood and quite a lot cleaner and quieter than back in the concrete canyons. I found my way to the Stanhope mansion with the help of a filling station attendant who had to look it up on a private sketch map.

It was an old, old house of many rooms, some of which, I was sure, would be in plain sight and others camouflaged and secret, maybe even equipped with secret panels and trap doors. To go with all this, the fortyish matron who let me in wore a black dress and a starched white collar and her hair in a tight bun at the back of her head. She had black, shrewd eyes and when I mentioned my name she nodded briskly.

"You're the detective," she said.

My eyebrows wiggled in spite of themselves.

"I'm a private detective, yes," I said.

"And you want to see Miss Dorothy Stanhope."

"If you say so."

"One moment, please."

She turned with military precision and went to a closed door on my left. I waited in the vast reception hall, looking up a circular staircase down which Scarlett O'Hara could have driven a spanking team, and suddenly I felt acutely conscious of the adhesive patch under my left eye, of a stiffness in my right knee, and of bruises here and there and the way my eyes puffed around the edges. At the top of the staircase was a setback upstairs hall, and ranged along the wall was a series of heroic size, full-length portraits of ancestors, mostly in military dress. They dated from 1776 to W.W. I and they looked like high brass, one and all. I looked at them for quite a while and when the door opened and the housekeeper signified I was to be admitted, I found myself limping.

I limped into a high-ceilinged, wood-paneled room, dominated by a fireplace with a marble hearth and mantel. It was totally in harmony with the Early American furnishings, no doubt worth a good deal more that day than when they had been purchased.

Confronting me was a couple, the female half of which was far and away the easier to look at. Miss Dorothy Stanhope was a breath-taking combination of "follow me" lusciousness and "down, boy" dignity. She had hair the color of daffodils, tightly curled in a close-fitting cap on her shapely head. Although full-bodied, with an appropriate distribution of flesh, bone and muscle, she had dressed herself to modify the extremes as to concave-convex. The effect was all the more heightened. In the cool, chaste gray dress, every move she made was a matter of instant record. Her face was strong, with a ruddy complexion; her eyes wide-set, greenish and mobile, her mouth scarlet and a little stiff. I noted, too, that except for the color of her hair, she was the girl in the picture I had snitched.

She shifted her position to greet me without rising, but when she spoke it was definitely "down, boy."

"What kind of detective are you, Mr.—?"

"Mac," I said. "A private one."

"Would you care for a drink?"

"No, thanks."

"Tea, coffee, a glass of milk?"

"Nothing, thanks."

"This is Mr. Hayes," she said, gesturing toward the guy in the elegant Ivy League suit. "Foster Hayes."

Mr. Hayes and I bowed to each other. Miss Stanhope crossed her legs, smoothed her chaste skirt over her careful knees and nodded permission for me to sit down.

"Are you one of these detectives who goes around getting dirty secrets out of people?" she asked.

"It depends," I said, feeling very tired, "on how much there is in it. For me, I mean."

Miss Stanhope was busy lighting a cigarette. Mr. Hayes had been willing, even eager to light it for her, but his machine hadn't taken fire on the first try and by the time he got it going, Miss Stanhope had helped herself. Mr. Hayes frowned, cleared his throat and looked at me sternly.

"I'm sure you will understand," he said, "that Miss Stanhope and I were in the midst of a rather important discussion—"

Miss Stanhope cut in.

"The reason I asked," she said, "was because you look as if you might have run afoul of a desperate husband—or lover?"

I touched the bandage on my cheek.

"No," I said, "I was in an explosion. Luckily I was only on the edge of it. The person in the middle was a young and lovely woman named Mrs. Barry Henley. She is now dead—that is, what they were able to find of her. I was very fond of her."

"I'm sorry," Miss Stanhope said.

She put her hand over her face, but I couldn't tell whether she felt shock or was just yawning. I glanced at Mr. Hayes, then looked away quickly so as not to encourage him. He looked quite a lot like a currently high-placed government official and I kept expecting him to make a speech.

"It's in connection with Mrs. Henley's murder that I have come to see you," I said.

She took her hand down and rested it on her thigh. Mr. Hayes's eyebrows bobbed about like mechanical brushes.

"She was murdered?" Miss Stanhope said.

"The explosion involved her automobile," I explained. "It too was a total loss."

"I seem to keep saying the wrong thing," she said, snuffing out her cigarette. "Please go ahead. What do you want from me?"

"I'm not sure. About a year ago, Mrs. Henley's husband died, also violently. His name was Barry Henley and he was a private detective, too. I believe that at the time of his death he was employed by your father."

Mr. Hayes decided the time had come to assert himself. He rose to his full, substantial, all-American height of about six feet, three inches, packed in a two-hundred-pound frame of what appeared to be solid meat without lumps or sags.

"Now, see here," he said, using both his mouth and his eyebrows, "if your investigation touches on intimate matters involving the Stanhope family—"

"Shut up, Foster," Miss Stanhope said, "and sit down."

She smiled at me for the first time. It was quite a thing.

"My father has been dead for almost a year," she said gently, "and I was away for quite a while—"

"Yes," I said, "but you did come home before he died and I thought you might have an idea why he hired Barry Henley."

Foster Hayes was impatient.

"Dorothy, I think we ought to consult before—" She waved him to silence.

"I'm glad to co-operate," she said. "I do remember vaguely that Mr. Henley was doing something for my father. I don't know exactly what it was. After my father died, we received a bill for Mr. Henley's services. We paid it. I never met Mr. Henley myself and I never discussed him with my father."

It was pretty straightforward. I had no immediate follow-up in mind and I got to watching Mr. Hayes's fascinating eyebrows.

"I'm very sorry to hear that Mrs. Henley had such a tragic life," Miss Stanhope said.

"Yes," I said. "Well, it didn't last too long. It was pretty hard on her to lose her husband so soon after they were married. Nobody has the honor to be your husband, I take it?"

"No," she said, lighting another cigarette. "Foster would like to be, wouldn't you, dear? But we haven't come to terms yet."

It was now Foster Hayes's turn to call on his dignity. He did it quite well, I thought, and I decided to give him a gold star for effort. He rose to his height again, dusted his hands lightly, smiled rather thinly toward me and leaned down to kiss Miss Stanhope's forehead.

"'Bye, dear," he said, "I'll run along. I can see you would rather be alone with—Mac?"

Miss Stanhope smiled perfunctorily and took a long, non-perfunctory drag on her cigarette. I removed Mr. Hayes's gold star from his chart and Mr. Hayes removed himself from the room quietly, in a genteel way that was not without a certain style.

There was some silence. Miss Stanhope drew a deep breath, inflating the cool fabric at her bosom in a high-class way. I anticipated her next move and was across the room with a lighted match by the time she had the cigarette well tamped. She would damn well be in my debt for something. She looked up at me while she sucked it to life, her face symmetrically hollowed. At close range I saw that what had appeared at a distance to be a flawless, creamy pink complexion was really an expertly applied commercial face.

"Thanks," she said, blowing delicate smoke.

"Sure."

"I'm sorry I was rude to you. Foster brings out the female dog in me."

I let it go by. It went in a hurry, but it came back.

"I oughtn't to feel that way," she said. "Foster has been immensely kind to me. He is an immensely good man. And in a couple of years he will be chairman of the board of the Stanhope Steel Company."

This girl doesn't have anyone to talk to, I thought. Why me?

"Well, Miss Stanhope," I said, "I am not the chairman of anybody's board. Maybe you and Mr. Hayes can work something out."

"Touché," she said quietly.

There was a discreet tap at the door.

"Yes?" Miss Stanhope said.

The housekeeper looked in. She was wearing a heavy cloth overcoat, a hat and rather chic gloves. She looked determined, rather like a busy pigeon.

"I'm going to the market now," she said.

"All right, Brenda," Miss Stanhope said. "Brenda—Miss Lundquist— may I present a private detective named Mac? Miss Lundquist is my faithful friend and housekeeper."

"We have met; how do you do?" Miss Lundquist said.

"Oh?"

"He introduced himself when he came in," Brenda said.

"I see."

In a precise manner, clickingly, as if the words were attached to a continuous ribbon and she was snipping them off as they came to maturity, Miss Lundquist said, "After I leave the market I must go to the drugstore—the Village Drug, that is."

"All right, Brenda," Miss Stanhope said.

"Is there anything I might bring you from the Village Drug?"

"No, thank you."

I repeated it mentally several times: Village Drug, Village Drug.

"If I should be late getting back," Brenda insisted, "there's a luncheon menu in pans in the refrigerator. All it needs is to be set on the stove and heated slowly."

"Thank you, Brenda," Miss Stanhope said.

"I may be longer than usual."

"All right."

Brenda made her exit with determined, quick, pigeon steps. Dorothy Stanhope drew deeply on her cigarette, put her head back, closed her eyes and exhaled a long, steady smoke trail from between her teeth.

Village Drug, I thought.

I got up and paced the floor, examining the handsome old room.

"It's quite a place," I said. "Your family built it?"

"No," she said. "We came here from the East—from Boston. We were about four. It was because of the war and my father's position in the steel business. There wasn't much housing then, I guess, and there was this old place that could be bought. My father bought it. After the war he wasn't well and there was nobody else to consider, except Carolyn and me, so he stayed on here. If you're interested in old houses, you might like to take the tour."

"Thanks," I said. "One of these days. You mentioned someone named Carolyn."

"My twin sister, Carolyn. My mother died just before we moved here."

"Your sister lives here too?"

She had put out her cigarette and now she smiled a little ruefully and smoothed her skirt over her knees. "Not exactly," she said. "You see—Carolyn is something of a problem."

"Enough of a problem to hire a private detective to keep his eye on her?" I said. "Or to find her if she should wander off?"

Her hands tightened on her knees and she closed her eyes for a moment, then opened them wide. It was to become a recognizable mannerism.

"Well," she said, with another of those smiles, "I guess I walked right into that one, didn't I?"

I took the 4x5 print out of my pocket, crossed the room and showed it to her. She looked at it calmly. "That's Carolyn," she said.

"Identical twins?"

She nodded.

"For a long time we considered tossing a coin to see which one ought to be tattooed or something, so Father could tell us apart."

I put the photo in my pocket.

"Where did you get it?" she asked.

"From Barry Henley's file," I said. "There were several copies, as if maybe he had them for identification purposes. He would spread them around here and there, you understand, in the hope that someone would recognize Carolyn—"

"I understand."

She put a strong period there. She was through talking about Carolyn. I had thought we were making progress, but it looked as if I would have to start over to open things up.

"What I'm trying to do," I said, "is to reconstruct certain aspects of the past. In order to find a motive for Virgie Henley's murder, I have to pick up the threads of Barry's year-old investigation and try to go on with it."

She frowned and chewed her lip.

"Sounds complicated," she said. "And dangerous."

"Maybe."

"What if you pick up Mr. Henley's threads and wind up the same way he did—dead?"

"Well, everybody dies."

The doorbell rang. Miss Stanhope looked annoyed. She put out her cigarette and got up, saying, "Please excuse me."

"Of course."

She went out to the front hall, closing the door behind her. I heard the door open, then close quietly. I heard nothing more for quite a while and then I went over and put my ear to the door.

I heard a low, taut, feminine whisper. Then another—lower, gruff, peremptory. I couldn't make out any words. The whispering went on, back and forth, increasing in intensity. It sounded like an argument all right, but it might have been with a grocery boy or a Fuller Brush man, only Fuller Brush men don't ordinarily deliver their pitches in whispers. I began to listen in earnest.

There was a sudden sharp, feminine squeal, not quite suppressed, and a furious "No! Take your hands off me—" I went out there. Miss Stanhope was angry-red in the face. The man who was holding her arms, in what must have been a painful, twisting grip, was Brophy's young hand, Mr. America.

"Let go!" Miss Stanhope said for the tenth time.

The youngster was glaring at me, attending to her only with his hands. She twisted, trying to free herself, and he tightened the grip till she gasped lightly. I tossed my hat aside.

"Let her go," I said.

"What's he doing here?" the kid said, snarling.

"Let the lady go now," I said, rearranging my weight.

He looked a little murder at me, then pushed her back out of the way. I heard her fall, not too heavily. The boy pivoted to get at me and it could have been pretty bad, but this time I had him in front of me and we were alone—virtually.

I fell back enough to pull him off balance and hit him in the midsection. He grunted and swung one. It was a hard drive, but I managed to duck it and he was looking for me. I crowded him against the front wall, grabbed a handful of hair and banged his head, then let go and got away. He shook his head like an irritated dog and charged me. I wouldn't have had a chance against his youth and strength except that he had got careless and off balance. He came too fast. I stuck a foot in his way and gave him a push in the small of his back. He stumbled onto the stairs. Miss Stanhope jumped out of the way.

He was down then and I caught both his hands and brought them up in back, high enough to make him cuss, and held onto them while he got to his feet. I pushed him to the door and put a little more pressure on the hammerlock.

"Goodbye now," I said.

I stepped back and released him experimentally. He stood with his back to me, shifting his coat on his shoulders and shooting his cuffs. I stayed out of reach in case he should turn on me. He didn't, probably because he didn't want to carry it any further in this location. There would be other places, other times. I wished it could be otherwise. He could kill me easy.

He opened the door and paused to look back.

"You know this man?" I asked her.

"I never saw him before in my life," she said, spitting the words like dirt out of her pretty mouth.

The kid made a face, shrugged and left us. I watched by one of the glass panels beside the door while he walked to the drive, climbed into a powder-blue sedan and drove away. Then I turned around and looked at Miss Stanhope. She was massaging her arm where he had held her. She glanced at me, then looked down at her right foot, which was drawing a small circle on the Oriental carpet.

"Thank you," she said. "I can't imagine what possessed him—"

"Never saw him before in your life?" I said.

She looked at me sharply.

"No," she said.

"Do you get a lot of guys like that, ring your doorbell and grab you? Not that they wouldn't want to, but—"

"That's enough," she said.

"Maybe he mistook you for your sister, Carolyn."

"Maybe."

"Only she's a brunette. You're a blonde."

"Yes. Or she was the last time I saw her."

"You don't see her often?"

"Very seldom. She lives—elsewhere."

"Do you know where she's living now?"

"No."

"Do you have her last previous address?"

"No."

I looked at her for a while. She softened some, spread her hands.

"I know it must sound awfully strange, but Carolyn is—well, she's a strange girl. We don't really have anything to do with each other any more."

"Does she work? Is she on an allowance?"

"She works sometimes. She sings in—places—supper clubs, you know? She sings rather well. Jazz."

"You don't know where she's working now?"

"No—she changes frequently."

She put her hands to her head and squeezed.

"Hadn't you better sit down?" I asked.

"No, I'll be all right. You'll have to excuse me now."

"What if our friend comes back? Do you have any way to protect yourself?"

"I'll be all right," she said.

"I plan to come back and have another talk with you," I said.

She looked at me hard and stubborn for about a minute. Then she smiled a little, giving in.

"Very well, I guess I owe you that much."

"You don't owe me anything. I'd have done the same for someone else. But maybe you owe Barry Henley's widow something."

She put her lip between her teeth. Her hands twisted at her skirt. She was a beautiful woman with a tough core, and no matter how irritating the type can be, it draws you. I wouldn't have said we would ever be friends, but I thought maybe we could get the job done without loss of respect on either side.

"All right for now," I said. "If you want some free advice, I'd suggest you keep the doors locked and the chain set."

"It's good advice. Thank you."

I started away and she watched me every step. I knew because I was watching too. She let me get through the door and halfway down the front steps, then she said, "No—wait!"

I waited.

"Yes?" I said.

She came to the top of the steps and hovered there with her hands open and her face a question, like a tormented angel. Or, could be, devil. It wasn't clear which.

"Don't hold it back, Miss Stanhope," I said, "if it hurts."

She cleared her face with some effort and settled back squarely on her feet.

"No," she said. "It's nothing. Goodbye."

She turned her back on me and went into the house.

I drove to the village shopping center in Riverwood and found the Village Drug. Parked across the street, I watched it. After a while a little German car pulled up in front and Miss Lundquist got out. She walked with those quick, birdlike steps across the walk and into the store.

I sat there for a while, then punched my starter and got away quietly. It could be that I was passing up a vital handout of information. But it could be, too, that over the long haul, a little advance in pressure would spill the dam wide open.

CHAPTER NINE

In Donovan's office they were having a conference. It appeared for a few minutes that I wouldn't be admitted. Then Donovan looked out to say something to the guy responsible for his privacy and nodded me in.

There were six of them. There was a guy from the lab. Sergeant Monday was there. I took off my hat and sat down to one side, so as not to insinuate myself into the group, and proceeded to mind my own business. I wasn't all the way in tune with their conversation and had to put things together as it went along. Donovan tossed me a big manila envelope full of photographs.

"Way they pieced things together," he said. "If you want to take a look."

I didn't want to. I held the envelope on my lap, listening in. They were talking about the dynamite used in rigging Virgie's car. They talked about it for quite a while until Donovan broke in impatiently.

"Anybody can get dynamite," he said. "Check it out, sure. May take a couple of years. But let's not waste time in this room wonderin' how he got hold of the dynamite."

He looked at Sergeant Monday.

"You say Mrs. Henley identified Whisky Davis as one of the people came around her place."

"That's right," the Sergeant said. "Seemed pretty sure of it."

He glanced at me and I nodded.

"Anybody seen Whisky Davis lately?" Donovan asked.

I gave him a sign and he returned it negative, meaning I should stay out of it. Nobody else in the room had seen Whisky Davis lately.

"Check him out?" one of the plain-clothes dicks asked.

"Let me think about it," Donovan said. "Did she identify anybody else at all out of them shots?"

"No," Sergeant Monday said.

"Not even maybe?"

"No, sir."

The guy from the lab got on his feet.

"You need anything more from me, Lieutenant?"

"No, go ahead," Donovan said.

He went out. Donovan nodded to another one in plain clothes and he went out too. That left five of us.

"It kind of looks like Brophy," Donovan said, "but it don't look real clear. I don't want to go shakin' him down and puttin' his back up till we got something. You start hangin' around askin' after Whisky Davis."

"I don't think Whisky does much on his own," Sergeant Monday said.

"He's a handle," Donovan said.

"Anything else, Lieutenant?"

"No," Donovan said.

Monday went out. The two remaining detectives were up.

"You want us to check out the Stanhope place?"

"Not yet," Donovan said. "Get on the dynamite and see what there is to learn about Brophy and Whisky Davis. But don't get too close. We ain't ready yet."

They went out, crowding the doorway. It left me alone with Donovan. His telephone rang.

"Yeah, Donovan," he said. "Yeah… Who?… Well, tell it to the Captain. Don't tell me. I can't do nothin' for you."

He hung up.

"You saw Brophy this mornin'?" he asked.

I told him about it.

"What do you think?" he asked.

"I think Brophy was looking for something in the Henley apartment. I think it was probably Brophy that worked over the place after Virgie was dead. I don't have any idea whether he had her killed. But it's a Brophy technique, with the dynamite and all."

"You're a big help."

"Thanks, Lieutenant. I don't have much except some pretty good questions."

"Go ahead."

"Number One: If there was something they wanted that bad out of Henley's place, with him dead for a year, why did they wait so long? Why not move in as soon as Barry was dead?"

"Tell me."

"It could be they didn't know what they wanted or why they wanted it until just now."

"So?" he said.

"So this might mean no direct connection between Henley's death and this search. So Henley might have died accidentally."

"All right," Donovan said, "go ahead."

"Number Two: Why kill Virgie? Even Brophy wouldn't knock somebody off just so he could look for something. It must have been because Virgie knew, or was thought to know, something confidential and valuable. It would probably be something she would have learned from Barry."

"What did she tell you?"

"Nothing that would explain anything. But they—whoever they are—don't know that."

He looked exasperated.

"So," I hastened to add, "she could have been killed merely because somebody thought she knew something that couldn't be let out. Just an insurance killing."

"Would have to be quite a big thing," Donovan said.

"Not necessarily. An inconsequential bit of information might stand in the way of something big."

"Like what?"

"I don't know."

"You went through Henley's files."

"I didn't find anything—with one possible exception. A guess."

"Like what?"

"In the Stanhope case—there may have been a will."

"No doubt."

"I mean a will with something funny about it."

"That Henley was in on?"

"It could be."

His phone rang again. This time it was the Captain.

"Yes, sir," Donovan said. "Yes, sir, I did… All right, sure. Right now?… I'm on the Henley case—the dynamiting, yeah. No, sir, nothin', not yet… All right, sir."

He hung up, scratched a laborious note on a pad and pushed it away on the desk.

"Did you go out to the Stanhope place?" he asked.

"I did."

"Who did you see?"

"A Miss Dorothy Stanhope, her boyfriend, a Foster Hayes, and a house-keeper named Brenda Lundquist."

"What about Miss Stanhope?"

"A rich girl, kind of worried."

"Worried about what?"

"I don't know yet. Family troubles maybe."

He looked at me for a while with suspicion. It was part of the job.

"I don't have to tell you, Sherlock," he said, "that the reason you're in this so far is only because you might be able to go in places where we can't go without a lot of fuss and bother."

"I understand," I said. "I appreciate it that you're giving me this big break, letting me put in my time free of charge and wear out my shoes and not putting a stop to it."

He cleared his throat, pursed up his mouth and looked around with a pained expression. He opened a top drawer, took out a small key and unlocked a bottom drawer in his desk. He took out a squat brass cuspidor and set it on the floor, gauging the distance carefully. Then he let fly. It made a good sharp pinging sound. He looked pleased. He picked up the cuspidor, put it back in the drawer, closed and locked it and put the key away.

"Goddam health department!" he said.

He eyed the envelope in my lap.

"You looked at those pictures?"

"I don't care to."

"There's nothin' of the lady in 'em. Wasn't enough of her really—"

"All right! I'll look at your goddam pictures!"

"Worth a million words," he said.

"Or nothing."

He nodded.

"Or nothin'."

There were several photographs: of pieces of the car, roughly assembled; enlarged microscopic studies of sections of tires and some vague-looking shots of what I took to be the traces on the pavement.

"I can't hardly wait," Donovan said, "for one of those cameras that'll take pictures of stuff when it ain't there any more. Think of the parking citations the boys will be writin'—"

"Spoken like one of Chicago's finest," I said.

I tossed him the envelope.

"These don't mean a thing to me," I said.

He looked a little disappointed, but shrugged and put them away in his desk.

"About this will," Donovan said.

"Only a hunch," I said. "I found some notes Henley had made and in one of them he referred to an emergency call to the Stanhope place, evidently to be a witness to something."

"Henley," he grumbled. "A year ago? That's a nice fresh lead. Did he mention any names of people still livin'?"

"Only a couple in the Stanhope family."

"I got some papers in the works to get at those files. Lawyer's probably got 'em all cleaned out by now."

"Maybe not. I'm having lunch with Budge. Want to come along?"

"Yeah."

His phone rang again and he grabbed it with a big hand.

"Yeah," he growled, "what?—oh, yes, sir. Yes, I'll be very careful... No, if it's all the same to you... All right, sir."

He hung up, swearing under his breath.

"Captain riding you?" I said.

He reached for his hat and jammed it on his head.

"Been botherin' around me for three days. Some psycho got sprung from the booby hatch and started issuin' statements: he's goin' to get Donovan, the lousy cop that sent him up. Goin' to cool me for keeps. Nobody can seem to locate him." He snorted. "Some punk with his big talk—killed his own kid, a baby, broke its neck with his own hands. Then he beat his wife to death with a flatiron."

"How did he get sprung?" I asked.

"You tell me. I already told the Captain to quit worryin', I got a private bodyguard."

"Yeah? Who?"

"You. You do that type of work, don't you?"

"Great. I'm not heeled."

"No?"

He opened his desk, took out a small, flat automatic and saw to its mechanism, then slid it into his pocket.

"Damn things," he said, "pull your pockets all out of shape."

"One precaution you might take," I said.

"Yeah?"

"Go easy on the potatoes. You make a hell of a target."

He muttered a few short words.

* * * *

I was to meet Budge at a men's grill on Clark Street. Donovan and I got there five or six minutes early and I bought a round of beers. It was too clattery for conversation. Fifteen minutes passed and I made a tour of the place, looking for Budge. He wasn't there.

"Must have got tied up in court," I said.

"What?"

I repeated it, louder. Donovan nodded and looked hungrily at the displayed entrees under the glass service counter.

"Let's eat," I said.

"Now you're talkin'."

Ordinarily a plain-clothes detective, even a famous old-timer like Donovan, is as anonymous as a parking meter. But it happened that day that three civilians recognized him and felt impelled to greet him and pass the time of day. Donovan was up and down, shaking hands and nodding and trying to remember their names. Halfway through the meal, he was red in the face, his corned beef and cabbage were cold, his beer warm and he was a badly frustrated man.

"Taxpayers," he grumbled.

"Uh-huh," I said. "Big ones."

"They're all the same to me."

He spoke the literal truth.

"Your man ain't goin' to show?"

"No," I said.

"I got to get to work."

I didn't try to hold him. In fact, I had to struggle to keep the impatience out of my face. This involved twinges of guilt. Because I had used the time left to me over the beers and Donovan's unexpected visitations to think about things, and I had suddenly and unexpectedly formed a complete and unified picture of why Barry Henley had died and his wife, Virgie, a year later, and of where the people concerned with it fitted in. I had to restrain myself from blurting it out on the spot. It had an impact on me that, within its minute scope, must have been comparable to the impact of relativity on Einstein. The only trouble with it was that I had no idea in the world why it was true. It would have to be checked out and there was no use giving it to Donovan now. He was interested in evidence.

CHAPTER TEN

We separated at Clark and Randolph and I walked over to Budge's office. He wasn't in. His associate, Eric Safford, was a big, youngish fellow with a crew cut, wearing a loafer jacket. His desk was piled with opened legal tomes. He looked up at me broodingly at first, then came to life when I told him my name.

"Oh, sure," he said, "come on in. Paul had to go to court out north. I phoned the restaurant about eleven-thirty."

"They must have fouled it up," I said.

"Sorry."

"No harm done. You're Safford?"

"Right."

He had a brisk, open-faced style, in the best current tradition of executive youth. All we have any more in this country—executives and bums. And private detectives, if you want to be charitable about it. He was looking at the tape on my face.

"You had a narrow one last night, huh?" he said.

"Narrow enough. Did Budge fill you in?"

"Pretty much."

"You'll get an order on those Henley files probably any minute."

He nodded. "We're expecting it."

"Have you been over this with Budge?"

"Those files? No, he only mentioned he had been through them with you at the storage company."

"Been long with Budge?" I said.

"About six months. I was lucky. I had to drop out of law school in my last year. Plan to finish at night school. Mr. Budge took me in, just about saved my life."

"It's a tough road nowadays," I said.

"You are so right. I did about everything in the world just to keep going. I've got union cards in half a dozen trades that I had to learn in order to eat."

I looked past him out the window and he slipped into a respectful silence.

"I was wondering," I said, "speaking of money, whether that estate's been settled yet. Guy Henley was working for."

"Oh, the Stanhope estate," he said.

"Uh-huh. It would have been a big one and the chances are it's still in probate."

"Easy enough to find out," he said.

"I thought you or Budge could find out quicker than I could, and some of the details, you know?"

"Glad to." He reached for the phone. "Want to wait for it?"

"No, thanks, no time. You could give me a ring here."

I tossed a card onto his desk. He glanced at it, stood up and held out his hand. We shook on it. He had a big, strong hand and a firm grip.

"Good luck," I said, "and thanks for digging out that dope for me."

"Nothing," he said.

I went out. I wasn't so sure Safford was the lucky one. This kid looked like a go-getter and Budge had never gotten what you could call rich and famous. Maybe he figured that they could make something together. Nothing takes the place of youth and drive.

* * * *

I drove home, parked in front of the office and opened my mail. Then I went out and walked around the car a couple of times, as earlier in the day. Finally I got in and drove to a filling station where I was known and left it to be serviced. I took a taxi back to the office. Nobody had rigged the taxi to blow up. Everything was going fine.

There were a few phone messages. One was from Foster Hayes at the Stanhope Steel Company in Whiting. I dialed the number and got put through to Mr. Hayes in a hurry.

"What can I do for you?" I asked him.

He spoke carefully and a little sternly.

"I think we ought to have a talk," he said.

"Sure. When?"

My ready acceptance seemed to throw him off the track. There was a pause. Then he said, "This afternoon?"

"All right, where?"

"Uh—Pump Room?"

"Why not? Can you get me in?"

"Certainly."

He said it with that unctuous inflection. He would make a dandy candidate for Vice President of the United States, I thought.

"Is that all?" I said.

"Yes, thank you. Four-thirty then at the Pump Room."

"Fine."

I could almost hear him telling his friends, with that cultivated air of mild amazement: "So I simply told him directly I wanted to have a talk with him and he said, 'Of course, at your convenience,' just like any other businessman. Imagine!"

There had been a call, too, from a nameless woman at a Riverwood number. I decided to let her wait a while longer. A third call had come from Donovan. It was an old one and I had probably seen him since, but to be on the safe side, I dialed. I hadn't quite finished when there was a knock at the door. I hung up and went over there.

It was my little redheaded nurse—in street clothes. She looked up at me shyly and her hands moved.

"I just wondered—" she said, "how you were feeling."

"Please come in."

She looked over her shoulder and peeked around past me and then she came in.

"So this is your office," she said.

"This is it. If you're here on business, I'll dazzle you with a series of lightning deductions about your private life and habits. All I need to know is your name."

She smiled. She had little white teeth between cute red lips, and freckles across her nose. She was all of twenty years old. I did not believe that she spent her free evenings hanging around taverns. I believed she probably had dates with medical students from Northwestern, or possibly football players.

"My name is Bonny," she said, "Bonny Thompson, and I don't have any private life."

"No time like the present," I said, "to get started. Sit down and I'll ply you with liquor."

"Oh, no—at this hour?"

"It's after noon."

"It's not five-thirty."

"You never take one till five-thirty?"

"Never."

You cute little braggart, I thought.

She sat down on the couch and locked her ankles together and pushed her skirt down over her knees.

"Working the night shift this week?" I asked.

"And next week too. I just started, you see, and I don't have much seniority."

"You don't have much seniority at anything I can think of," I said, "but I'm growing fonder of you every minute."

"You wouldn't be giving me a sweet-talking to, would you?" she said.

"I'm not above it."

She glanced around with feminine inquisitiveness. "It's very pleasant," she said.

"Well," I said, "you can hang your hat in it without having to grope for a hook."

She frowned a little, then smiled.

"That's a very good expression," she said. "Did you just now make it up?"

"I'm afraid I did."

"I think it's very good."

"Where did you come from?" I asked.

"You mean where is my home town?"

"Approximately."

"It's a little town not far from Springfield. I took my nurse's training at Illinois. Champaign."

"It shows," I said.

"Thank you, sir."

We looked at each other and at our feet.

"That was a bad cut you had on your face," she said. "How does it feel?"

"Oh, it's—" I thought it over. What the hell, I thought, a man's entitled. I patted the place and winced slightly.

"I don't know," I said. "Let's see."

I ripped off the Band-Aid and she gave a little start. I patted it some more. She jumped up and grabbed my hand, holding it.

"No!" she said. "Don't put your fingers on it for goodness' sake!"

"Excuse me," I said.

"Here, let me do it."

She got very busy for about three minutes and I wound up with a clean, absolutely sterile Band-Aid and a nice warm feeling.

Damned clever, old man, I told myself.

"Is that the only place you hurt?" she asked.

"I could think of more, but I don't want to push my luck."

She blushed and looked away. She walked to the window behind my desk and looked out at the street.

She was a girl who thought she ought not to stay any longer but didn't quite know how to say goodbye.

"There's something you ought to tell me," I said.

She gave that cute little jump again.

"There is?" she said.

"I think so."

She frowned.

"Didn't mean to make you cry."

"Oh, stop it!" she said. "There's something—I don't know."

"Suppose we blow a bubble with it and see what it gums up," I said.

"You're crazy!"

"All right."

"Well, I keep thinking about last night. The—it—the explosion happened in front of two-seventeen, didn't it?"

"Uh-huh."

"That's where I live. I left for work about ten o'clock last night. When I went outside there was a truck out in the street with its motor running. There was a mechanic working on the car that was parked right in front. I didn't pay much attention. Like the Lieutenant said—"

"No attention at all?"

"I'm afraid not, but I might know the truck if I saw it again."

"Was it a regular service truck, with a name painted on it—Auto Club or something—?"

"No, just an ordinary dark-colored truck, open in the back like, what do you call it, a pickup?"

"Did you see the mechanic's face?"

"No, not really. Mostly I just saw his back bending over the motor."

"Was he big? Medium? Small?"

"Pretty big."

"Bigger than I?"

"Maybe a little, not much."

"Don't be patriotic. I'm big enough for me."

"He was pretty big."

"Young or old?"

"Young I thought. Not as old as—I mean—"

"Okay, honey, don't worry about these little slips."

She backed away to the door, flustered.

"That's all," she said. "I just wanted to tell you what I saw."

"I appreciate it. Will you tell me something else?"

"If I can."

"How come you didn't tell the Lieutenant about it last night?"

She swiveled her eyes away.

"For one thing," she said, "I was sort of scared. I was afraid if I told him, he'd ask me a lot of questions I couldn't answer and—make me feel silly, you know?"

"Uh-huh?"

"Then I recognized you and I—well, I thought if you told him yourself it would mean more to him."

"I see."

"Well," she said, "I guess that's all."

"I hope not."

"What?"

"I hope we can get together again soon."

"Oh," she said. "Yes, I guess so."

She drifted out like an errant leaf and winter returned to the room. I looked at my watch and there was an hour in which I might get some rest before it was time to meet Mr. Hayes. I had my shoes off and my tie loosened when the telephone rang and five minutes of my rest period went into a conversation with Eric Safford in Paul Budge's office.

"About the Stanhope estate," he said.

"Yes?"

"This is confidential. It will come out at about two million dollars. Liquid assets, that is. There are some other miscellaneous holdings, real estate and such."

"Two million in cash. Who gets it?"

"Dorothy Stanhope. She's the daughter."

"What about Carolyn?"

"Who?"

"Carolyn, the twin sister."

"I wouldn't know. You understand, I didn't see any documents. It was just what I could squeeze out of my informant."

"I see. What was the date of the will?"

"I don't know that exactly, but it was probably drawn several years ago. Executor is a bank."

"And the whole two million goes to Dorothy without strings?"

"That's the way it looks."

"When will it come out?"

"Any day now. My informant thought it might be this week."

"How long has it been in probate?"

"Almost a year. That's usual."

"Uh-huh. Well, thanks. You have any ideas on it?"

"What kind of ideas?"

"I don't know—in connection with Henley or his widow?"

"I'm afraid not. You see, I didn't know the Henleys. Paul was the one—"

"All right."

"I heard from Paul. He said to tell you he was very sorry to miss the luncheon appointment and he'd like to see you as soon as possible. Maybe today?"

"Maybe. I'll see. Thanks for looking up the dope."

"Not at all. Nice talking to you."

I hung up. The kid was on the ball, I thought. Had nice manners, too. Budge might go a long way with that kind of help, if he would treat it right.

I thought about what he had told me about the Stanhope estate, and while it didn't solve the problem in one glorious swoop, it fitted into my theory all right. It was something to drive a peg with. I turned back the top spread on the studio couch, started to crawl in—and somebody knocked at my door.

I was going to let it go, then I thought it might be my redheaded sweetheart coming back and I climbed out and went to the door in my stocking feet.

It was Brenda Lundquist, the Stanhope housekeeper. She looked more like a pigeon than ever, in a tight-fitting, tailored suit and a swept-back hat with a single feather standing stiffly on one side, and her chest out and up.

Her eyes accused me.

"You didn't meet me at the Village Drug," she said.

"No, ma'am. I'm sorry. Won't you come in?"

She came in.

"I'm sure you understood what I was trying to tell you," she said. "You looked at me as if you did."

"I did but I was unable to get there in time. By the time I got to the Village Drug, you were gone." She sniffed and looked around the office with some distaste. She looked down at my shoeless feet and managed to refrain from sniffing.

"Sorry, I was just changing my shoes," I said.

"It's all right."

She sat in a chair and waited while I got my shoes on. I didn't bother with the tie.

"What was it you wanted to tell me?" I asked.

She nailed me with her birdlike eyes.

"It's about that Barry Henley thing, isn't it?" she said. "That young private detective?"

I shrugged into my jacket.

"What do you mean by 'that Barry Henley thing'?" I asked.

"I read about his widow dying in that explosion last night. I knew that was why you came to see Miss Stanhope."

"Oh."

"Because of Mr. Stanhope's hiring that detective a year ago."

"Yes. What was Henley expected to do for Mr. Stanhope?"

"It was a confidential matter," she said. "Even Miss Stanhope didn't know about it until after her father's death and then only vaguely."

I waited. My rest period was evaporating before my eyes. She had come prepared to tell me her story. It was clear in the way she pulled herself together under the tight-laced suit, in the firm decision of her mouth, a straight double line under her rather wide nose. She made it clear, too, that it was not without a struggle that she had reached her decision.

"It had to do with some of Mr. Stanhope's investments. He was interested in a new company that had sprung up after the war, an electronics concern. He had reason to believe that some of the firm's officers were less than straightforward and he wanted to check on them quietly. Mr. Henley was expected to look into it."

"Did Mr. Henley turn up anything that you know of?"

"He reported to Mr. Stanhope on several occasions. I wasn't a party to their talks so I couldn't say what Mr. Henley accomplished, if anything."

"Well, I don't want to seem suspicious, Miss Lundquist, but if you weren't a party to their conversations, how did you know about the original assignment?"

"Mr. Stanhope told me about that. Not that he took me into his confidence regularly, but—Mr. Stanhope was subject to moods. He often made rather impulsive decisions. Out of a clear sky, he would announce something—of course, he wasn't a young man. Anyway, he told me about these suspicions. 'Brenda,' he said, 'I think those characters over at Western Electronics are trying to bamboozle me.' Actually he didn't call them characters, he used another word. And he didn't exactly say bamboozle."

I nodded in understanding.

"Then he handed me a sheet of paper on which he had written Mr. Henley's name and telephone number. He asked me to call him and ask him to come and see Mr. Stanhope."

"And you called Henley?"

"No. As it turned out, I hadn't got around to doing it before Mr. Stanhope changed his mind and decided to do it himself."

"Did you hear the conversation?"

"But he had already told me why he wanted to see Mr. Henley."

"And that was what Henley was working on: Western Electronics. To see who was rigging the books?"

"Yes. That was it. I came to tell you—I would have told you at the Village Drug, and it would have been more convenient for me—because Miss Stanhope didn't know about it and I knew you wouldn't learn anything from her and she might get upset, having a detective call like that. Besides, I think it's just horrible what happened to that poor woman last night, and anything I can do to help clear up the mystery—you understand."

I nodded. I looked out the window. I scratched my nose with a couple of fingers and turned my chair a little and ran the toe of my shoe over the right-hand wall of the kneehole in my desk and finally I looked at Brenda Lundquist, who was sitting straight and pigeon-like on the stiff chair, with her hands on a black purse in her lap and her somewhat overdeveloped ankles crossed in a ladylike fashion.

"You're devoted to Miss Stanhope, aren't you?" I said.

"I've been taking care of her ever since she was a little girl," she said with pride.

"You would go out of your way to protect her from embarrassment or humiliation, wouldn't you, Miss Lundquist?"

"I don't know what you mean by that," she said stiffly.

I smiled at her.

"You did very good," I said. "I sort of admire you for it. But isn't it true, ma'am, that what Barry Henley really had to do was concerned with Miss Stanhope's sister, Carolyn?"

She stared at me.

"Let me relieve your mind," I said. "Miss Stanhope told me about her sister. Rather frankly."

Her lips moved soundlessly for a moment.

"What did she tell you?" she said then.

"Not an awful lot," I said, "but enough. She told me that Carolyn was her identical twin and that she had always been, as she put it, a problem."

"She told you that?" Miss Lundquist said quietly.

"Yes, ma'am."

She looked down at her hands and her fingers curled and opened and curled again in the black gloves.

"I see," she said. "I didn't realize that."

"You couldn't have known. I should have told you myself before you started on the other."

"No," she said. "It's all right. I should have known better."

"You were right to make the try," I said. "Maybe you would tell me something."

"Maybe."

"On a certain afternoon, some time after Barry Henley had taken on the Stanhope assignment, he was called to the Stanhope residence urgently. While he was there he acted as a witness to—something. Can you tell me what it was?"

"I think not."

"It was a new will, wasn't it?" I suggested.

Her mouth firmed up against me.

"Weren't you also one of the witnesses? Along with Barry Henley?"

No answer.

"What was in Mr. Stanhope's mind? Did he cut Carolyn off without an inheritance?"

Silence.

"But he had already done that, hadn't he, in the earlier will, the one that's about to come out of probate?"

I glanced at her closed, loyal face and went on, not because I expected any answers, but because sometimes if you go on theorizing long enough, you can draw an impulsive correction. Of course, you have to strike a sensitive nerve.

"Or maybe it was Dorothy he meant to cut off."

"No!"

I had struck the nerve all right, but I wasn't sure how. I looked at her and her eyes fell.

"You don't understand—" she said.

"I know I don't, but I'm trying. I've got a picture in my mind of an old, sick man trying to provide for a couple of daughters—either wisely or vindictively. A sick old guy whose friends have died or drifted away, so there's nobody around any more he can really trust, aside from the bank.

"He was worried about the way things were going with his family. His wild daughter Carolyn was in trouble; or maybe she had just run off and he wanted to find her, bring her home. Her sister, Dorothy, was away in the East. Were you with her, Miss Lundquist?"

She blinked and her mouth opened.

"What?" she said.

"Never mind. I'll go ahead, with your permission. The way it looks— Mr. Stanhope sent for Dorothy to come home and he hired a skip tracer to find Carolyn and set up communications with her. He hired Barry Henley.

"I can't account for the fact that Henley was looking for Carolyn all that time—something like three months. If it's true, as Dorothy told me, that she sings in night clubs—"

"It's true," she whispered.

"And if she was singing somewhere in town at that time, he ought to have found her within about forty-eight hours. But maybe she was on and off. Anyway, what I'm getting to, Henley must have conducted himself in a way that won Mr. Stanhope's respect and confidence."

I gave her time but she let it go. She would not again subject herself to contradiction. I couldn't hold it against her.

"I'm sorry you came all this way," I said, "to such little purpose. I would like to ask you one more question, or maybe two."

"What?" she said.

"You are in touch with Carolyn Stanhope from time to time, are you not?"

For a while I thought she was going to pass that one, too, but finally, with a slight nod, she said, "Yes, once in a while."

"Recently?" I asked.

"Not for two or three weeks."

"Did she tell you where she was working?"

Miss Lundquist's lips went into that cramp.

"I will find her," I said, "if she hasn't left the country. She's all I have that connects directly with Barry Henley. I'll find her whether you help me or not, but you can see that the easier it is to find her, the better mood I'll be in when the time comes."

She looked at me for about half a minute. Then, with a kind of ultimate weariness, she gathered her purse into her gloved hands and got up. She went to the door and I sat where I was, waiting. She opened the door and rested her forehead against it for a while and then she looked at me and said, "She's working at the 401 Club on Rush Street."

I got up.

"Thank you," I said. "May I see you to your car?"

"Don't bother," she said. "I can find my way."

I let her go.

There wasn't enough time left for a nap, but enough for a shower. I took it hot and cold and it helped some. Aside from the bruised and beaten feeling from the night before, I felt pretty good. I had learned some things. Nothing I had learned was at odds with the flash of insight I had experienced at lunch with Donovan.

CHAPTER ELEVEN

In the cool, quiet, glittering peace of the Pump Room, I faced Foster Hayes across a small table. I can say for him that he did not beat around the bush.

"What is it you want from Dorothy Stanhope?" he said.

I savored my high-class Martini and thanked him for it.

"Information," I said.

"Did you get it this morning?"

"Not enough of it."

He did away with some of his own Martini.

"Do you plan to go back for more?"

"Unless Miss Stanhope comes to me, I see no alternative."

"Surely you can't believe Dorothy had anything to do with those—deaths."

"Murders," I insisted.

"Very well."

"Probably she didn't," I said, "but it's—like opening a door suddenly and bashing somebody in the head: if you used a key to unlock the door, it's not the key that did the bashing, but you couldn't have opened the door—"

He gestured impatiently (and rightly).

"All right! I get the point. What I want to find out is whom are you trying to hit with the door?"

The dialogue was getting a little fancy and it was my own fault. But that didn't help any.

"That's not the way an investigation works," I said sternly. "If I knew who—or whom—I wouldn't need to bother Miss Stanhope. And, of course, I wouldn't be sitting around the Pump Room enjoying this exquisite Martini."

This was kind of underhanded of me. Because I had a pretty good idea where we were going, and by helping him to think I was impressed by these surroundings (which I somewhat was) I was pushing him in order to get there sooner and get it over with. But I was tired and short on scruples.

Anyway, he took the bait good. He ordered another round first, permitting me to buy, which was cagey of him. As we settled back with the Martinis—they were dry as a desert wind and cold as December—he asked, without looking at me, "May I ask if you are getting paid for this work you're doing?"

That was a dirty, unfair remark and took me by surprise. A man's non-commercial impulses are his own private affair, by God!

"Certainly," I said. "Hell, yes!"

"Sorry," he muttered.

"Okay. Excuse me for flying off the handle."

He made a "no hard feelings" gesture.

"Well," he said, "everybody can use extra money from time to time."

"I guess so."

"It's worth a good deal to me to have Dorothy left in peace."

I squinted at the olive in my Martini. It became two olives. I held it like that.

"It's worth a thousand dollars," he said.

I changed the focus of my eyes slowly and the two olives became one again.

"Five thousand I meant to say," Hayes said.

I lifted my glass. I didn't like to look at him any more.

"Well—?" he said.

I finished my Martini, set the glass down and made sure I had enough covering the tab to provide a substantial tip; because for all I knew I might have another chance sometime to be bought off in the Pump Room.

"Tell the truth," I said, "I'm actually more interested in Carolyn than Dorothy. How much would it be worth for me to lay off her too?"

He had pretty good character, at that. He didn't start apologizing. He sat there and kept his mouth shut while I got up and walked away. I would have said goodbye but I didn't want to spoil his mood.

It was the rush hour and it took me an hour and ten minutes to get home. I took off my clothes, showered and shaved, set my alarm for ten o'clock and went to bed. It was warm and soothing and lonely and black and wonderful.

* * * *

The 401 Club was like a hundred others in its class, maybe a little more elaborate. This was a shame because that made it more expensive to operate and it wasn't doing any business. Saturday night and after eleven o'clock and there weren't enough customers to pay the gas bill for three days.

A young couple at the only occupied table got up and left soon after I came in. There were two men at the small bar. I made a third. Two cocktail waitresses were standing in a corner, smoking and yawning. On a small platform beyond the bar a young fellow was fooling around on a spinet piano. There was a microphone on a stand. The lights were low, the music idle and wandering. I got the eerie feeling that everybody in the place was about to go to sleep for a thousand years. Except for the bartender.

The drink was pretty good, considering its source. Good whisky and not too much water. And without conversation—indication of a well-run place. Conversation was up to the customer.

The two customers farther along the bar were conversing quietly and in low tones. Then one of the waitresses wandered within their range and one of the guys caught her eye and said, "What time you get off, honey?"

"Thirty days from Tuesday," she said.

They both chuckled.

"I always like to hear her say it," one of them said. "I wonder where she got it?"

"Hey," the other one said and the bartender paid attention. "Let me know just before the chanteuse comes on, huh? So we can leave quietly. Don't want to hurt anybody's feelings."

The other customer laughed again. The bartender shrugged and walked away.

A few minutes passed silently and the two of them climbed down and went away. The piano player had disappeared. The bartender glanced at me and then looked toward the two who were leaving, almost out of sight now.

"There's an awful lot of people," he said, "walking around that could be making millions on the TV. Comics, you know?"

"I know," I said.

"It just seems like a cryin' shame that all that talent has to go to waste."

"It sure does."

I drained my glass and ordered another.

"Speaking of talent," I said, "who's your vocalist?"

He looked at me warily and I guess I managed not to look like a comedian.

"Carol Stanley," he said.

"Do you like the way she sings?"

He shrugged, rang up my drink and tossed the tab on the bar.

"I like Dinah Shore," he said.

"Who doesn't?"

He grinned and went about his business.

"Is it your place?" I asked.

"Hell, I wouldn't have it."

A man in a tuxedo, stocky and with one of those athletic-club complexions, came out from somewhere behind the piano and took a stool down toward the end of the bar. He swept the empty room with a dreary gaze and looked at his watch. The bartender stood respectfully, watching him.

"Big night," he said.

"Ugh," the bartender said.

I nodded to the one in the tux.

"It's a nice place," I said.

He nodded in return.

"Buy the gentleman a drink," he said.

The bartender moved to get it.

"Thanks all the same," I said, "but only if you'll have one with me."

"I don't drink," the owner said. "I can't afford it."

I felt sympathetic.

"If I leave now," I said, "would you close up and save money?"

"Hell, stick around," he said. "We got entertainment and all that." He turned on his stool. "Hey, Toscanini!" he called.

The piano player came out on the platform.

"Play something for the customer." He turned to me. "What do you want him to play? He can play anything."

"I don't care—what he feels like."

"He don't ever feel like it, but he'll do it."

The pianist sat down and fingered the keys and then played "Tea for Two." He played it very damn well. I acknowledged by lifting my glass and bought the piano player a drink. He played another number.

"He's good," I told the owner.

"I guess so. He knows some other pieces, too."

This was a badly disgruntled man.

The piano player was on his feet, adjusting the microphone, moving it out to the center of the platform. He signaled the bartender, who pushed a switch. A spotlight came on. The piano player moved the microphone a little more, then went to the bench, sat down and rubbed his hands for a while. The tendons in my wrists were drawn tight and I had an ache in the small of my back.

"Pretty generous," I said, "for her to come out and sing for one customer."

He gave me one of those looks.

"The tough thing," he said, "is to make her quit." The piano player struck a couple of chords, then went into a vamp of a current hit. I was watching the door when she came out. She was wearing a skintight peekaboo sheath, black with sequins. She looked good in it. Her hair was blue-black in the strong light. She was the spitting image of her sister, Dorothy, except for the hair, and except that she was maybe filled out a little more. But that could have been illusion, and Dorothy had been dressed differently. Her face was chalk-white and dead-pan. She stood there for several bars of the vamp, tapping one toe, getting the beat. Then she started to sing.

She was not any competition for Dinah, but she could carry a tune pretty well, and from time to time she exhibited a little style. It was something you could listen to without pain. Besides, she looked awfully good. You could forget the music and still be entertained. The sheath dress came up high enough to cover her lower breasts and there was an opaque strip across the crucial line. Then it was more or less transparent down to her navel, where there was another sequined patch; and then a larger one farther down. It was transparent down each side from her waist to her knee. She had a way of moving in rhythm that resulted in some interesting exhibition and naturally the stepped-up inhale-exhale lung action of the singing did fascinating things to her breasts. All in all, she put on a good show. When she finished the number, I applauded with considerable enthusiasm, breaking off suddenly when I caught the owner and the bartender looking at me.

"Didn't mean to be rowdy," I said.

"That's all right," the one in the tux said. "Let yourself go. Only thing, it always sounds funny to hear one person clapping all by himself. I don't know why but it always does."

"She's pretty good," I said. "What if she's not Helen Traubel, who needs singing?"

"Yeah," he said.

"I don't understand the empty house," I said. "Maybe if you could get her to combine a strip act with the song—wouldn't take much more than she's got now."

He looked very sour.

"I wouldn't dare," he said. "She came on here one night stark-naked. Pretty good crowd, too. No warning, the piano player had everything set, the light was on, and here she comes in her skin, absolutely. Had to be carried off."

"Is she on the stuff?" I asked.

"No, hell, no. She's just nuts."

We quit talking because she was into the next number, belting it out, as they say, with quite a lot of body English. When she came to the end and I had done the applauding bit again and she had acknowledged it with a breath-taking bow and had stepped back out of the light, the silence was a vacuum.

"If she's all that problem," I said quietly, "why do you keep her on?"

His face closed like a door closing.

"Contract," he said.

I let it go at that.

"Would it be against the rules for me to buy her a drink, after she finishes the set?"

He looked at the bartender and then at his watch and finally he said, "No, not exactly. But I wouldn't advise it."

I let that one go too. I was aware that some people were coming into the joint. One of the waitresses straightened quickly and primped at her hair. I watched while she paused beside the owner in his tuxedo. He put one hand on her shoulder and I heard him say, "Take good care of Mr. Brophy, honey, and watch your manners."

She shrugged away from his hand and moved out on the floor. The owner got down and straightened his tux and followed her. I looked around carefully.

There were five of them at a table halfway back in the small room: two ladies and three men. The men were Brophy, Whisky Davis and Mr. America. The ladies were anonymous.

I waited till Carol(yn) Stan(hope)ley got well into her next number—she was now playing to the new group and not to me—and then I got down cautiously and went to the men's room. From its alcove I looked out and studied the layout and picked a place where I would be pretty well out of sight unless they should start looking around in earnest. It was a small table at one side of the platform, hidden from the room by a potted plant. I slid over there and the unoccupied waitress came over and took my order. I had an impulse to ask what time she got off, just to see whether she had any other answers, but I restrained it.

* * * *

The kid sang for about half an hour. The Brophy party was properly appreciative and not raucous. When she finished the set, she went over there and sat down with them. She sat with Brophy. He treated her with what appeared at a distance to be respect. I couldn't hear what they talked about. I did some thinking about the club owner's reaction to my questions. Maybe Brophy was in the talent business too. Or maybe he was throwing it in with his equipment. Buy a gross of Martini glasses and get a vocalist for three weeks. One thing, if she was there on a Brophy contract, there wouldn't be any escape clauses in it.

They stayed for fifteen or twenty minutes, then started to break up. Davis and the kid with the shoulders escorted their dates toward the front door. Brophy and Carolyn went back to the bar and disappeared from my view. But a couple of minutes later, from another angle, I could see Brophy and the club owner in a dim corner. Brophy had a wallet out and was counting some bills. He folded them over and handed them to the owner, who stuck them in his pocket.

A big switch. I wondered if it could be possible that Brophy was paying Carolyn's way.

Anything could be possible. I didn't like this thought, but it was more or less unavoidable.

Brophy went out and the place was a mausoleum again. The spotlight had been turned off and the piano player was gone. The waitress came up and I gave her a ten-dollar bill and asked her to invite Miss Stanley to have a drink with me.

"I don't know—" she said doubtfully.

"Worth a try," I said. "Need another ten?"

"It might help."

I gave it to her. What the hell, I thought. I can always get it back from Foster Hayes.

euWhen she came, she was wearing a light coat over the peekaboo dress. It didn't make too much difference. She stood there a minute looking at me without expression, and then she put on a big smile and sat down in the chair I was holding.

"What'll you have?" I asked.

"What've you got?"

She giggled.

"Champagne all right?" I said.

"Ooh, I like champagne."

"Well than we're even, because I like you."

"What a perfectly nice thing to say."

"What time do you get through here?"

"Thirty days from Tuesday," she said, giggling.

I ordered the champagne and when the waitress had gone I put my hand over Miss Stanley's. She looked at our hands and gave that giggle again. "You're a fast worker, huh?"

"No," I said. "I'm drawn to you."

"You like my voice?"

"I like it fine. But there's something—different about you—quality, style. You don't really belong in this world."

"Oh, yes I do!" she said, drawing her hand away. "This is just where I belong."

"If you say so."

We sat there. Her face had an empty, wiped-out look when quiet; different from Dorothy's mobile awareness. Arrested development, I decided.

The waitress brought the champagne in a hamper and left it to chill.

"Something to go with it?" I asked her. "Caviar, smoked oysters—"

"Ooh—all that for me?"

"Why not?"

I don't know why I felt I had to spend all that money, except that I didn't want her to rush off before I had settled on an approach.

"How long have you been working here?" I asked her.

"Oh, about six weeks."

"Like it?"

"I love it!"

"Even when the house is empty?"

"I wouldn't say it's empty. You're here."

"Thank you, ma'am."

We sat there for a while in one of those awful silences.

"What line are you in?" she asked.

"I beg your pardon?"

"What do you do for a living?"

"Oh, I'm a private investigator."

"A private eye? Ooh!"

"Ooh what?"

"I'll bet that's exciting. Tell me about it."

"It's exciting, and dangerous."

"You get mixed up with desperate criminals and all that?"

"Sometimes."

"Tell me something that happened to you."

"Well—"

The waitress came back and opened the champagne and I ordered some caviar. She poured the bubbly and disappeared, returning too soon with the caviar. There was a rush going on that Carolyn Stanhope might not have anything to do with. I could feel it like wind on the back of my neck. When I tasted the champagne it was too warm to serve.

"Go ahead," Carolyn said. "Tell me."

"Nothing very much has happened to me," I said. "I've had some friends in this business, though, who weren't so lucky."

"Oh?"

She was drinking the champagne with some gusto but ignoring the caviar.

"I remember one, just a young guy, named Barry Henley. About a year ago he was killed in a fall over on the west side."

She watched me with her empty face.

"That's real too bad," she said. "I'm sorry."

"Nobody has figured out exactly what happened. At the time he was working for some tycoon from Riverwood. Stanhope, I think the name was."

"Stanhope?" she said. "That's sort of like my name. Stanley. Carol Stanley."

"Come to think of it," I said.

It was like talking to a dog or a horse, everything one way. I filled her glass for the third time, mine for the second. Even as she picked it up I could feel her slipping away from me. I could think of no words that might hold her.

"I notice you're friendly with Brophy," I said.

I thought she blinked a couple of times at that one but I couldn't be sure. She had the glass up and she might have got some bubbles in her eyes.

"Do you know Mr. Brophy?" she said.

"Everybody knows Mr. Brophy."

"I guess so," she said.

She finished her champagne, holding the glass in both hands, cupped. Then she put it down and got up.

"Thanks just horribly," she said. "I have to run now. You come back again, huh?"

"Sure."

I got up quickly and she leaned over and kissed my cheek and giggled and then turned and ran off. I sat down and poured some more champagne and looked at it. I was looking at it when the club owner came around the potted plant and stood by the table with his thumb moving like a hitch-hiker's.

"Out," he said.

"What?" I said.

"I said *Out.* You had your champagne and your fun and I warned you. I don't want to be responsible for what happens. Out."

It was the liquor, I guess.

"You going to handle it personally?" I said.

The bartender came around the potted plant and there were the two of them.

"Okay," I said.

I found my hat and put it on and got on my feet. They stood around watching me. I looked at the bartender and said, "What time do you close up?"

They looked at each other. The bartender opened his mouth.

"Don't tell me," I said. "Thirty days from Tuesday."

"Good night," the owner said.

"Uh-huh," I said.

Outside I checked the time and it was about twelve-thirty. It would be a long wait. I wandered around the street for a while and found a drugstore. They were just closing the counter and there was coffee left in the glass bowls they made it in. I bought what they had and the girl put it in some paper containers for me. I nearly burned my hands off carrying them back to the car.

I walked down the alley beside the 401 Club and found that there was no egress from it. I brought my car down the street on the same side as the club and parked it. Then I got in with the coffee and sat there and waited. And waited and waited…

* * * *

At about 2:45 a.m. a taxi pulled up in front of the joint. The dim lights on the front of the building went out. Five minutes passed and the door opened and she came out. The piano player was with her. They stood there for a couple of minutes. Then the piano player waved to her and walked away up the street. Carolyn Stanhope climbed into the taxi and it pulled away. I went along behind.

He wasted no time. He made for Chicago Avenue, turned right and headed for Lake Shore Drive. He turned right onto the Drive, heading south, so the chances were we had a trip ahead of us. I had a couple of bad minutes until I remembered that I had had the thing serviced that day and there was plenty of gas. The long wait had been worth while. There was no traffic to speak of, but enough that I could tail the taxi without much chance of being noticed.

We went way out south, beyond Jackson Park. We left the Drive at 67th Street and made a couple of turns in a quiet residential neighborhood where everybody seemed to be bedded down. The houses were large, not new, and expensive. I was two blocks behind the taxi when it pulled in to the curb. I went on past it, catching the house number en route, and turned right two blocks beyond. I drifted around the block slowly, parked off the subject street and walked back to the house. The taxi had gone and there were lights inside the house. I went up the walk to the front porch, found a bell and leaned on it.

Carolyn Stanhope opened the door and peered out. There was no light on the porch. I slid my foot against the door silently and leaned in.

"Oh—it's you," she said.

"Yes. May I come in?"

"I don't think so. You followed me home?"

"I did."

"You're persistent."

"I have to talk to you. Yesterday I talked to your sister, Dorothy, and to Brenda Lundquist. It was Miss Lundquist who told me where you were working."

"It's pretty late, see, and I've been working—"

"I won't stay long. It's a matter of some importance."

"Well—if you won't stay long—" Reluctantly she stepped back, widening the entrance. I went in and she closed the door and walked away. She was wearing gold lamè Capri pants and a black sweater with a silk kerchief around her neck. In the more normal light of the house, her face looked less starchy than under the spot and her hair more lustrous and not quite so blue.

"So you know Sister Dorothy," she said.

"A little."

Her mouth twisted.

"Poor, good, sweet Dorothy," she said. "How is she?"

"She seems to be just fine."

"Did she tell you all about her disreputable little sister?"

"No. She seemed quite fond of you."

She turned to a bar near the fireplace.

"Would you like something?" she said.

"No, thanks."

"Did you know who I was when you were at the club tonight?"

"Yes."

"How did you know?"

"Miss Lundquist told me you were singing there. And once I saw you there wasn't any mistake about your identity. The likeness is amazing."

"Isn't it?" she said.

She had abandoned her B-girl manners and there was more life in her face.

"All right," she said with resignation. "What do you want from me?"

"Did you know Barry Henley?" I asked.

"That private detective you were telling me about? No."

"Never met him in your life?"

"Not that I know of. Should I?"

"You didn't know he was looking for you?"

"How would I know that, unless he found me?"

"I thought he had found you."

"Well, who says I was lost?"

She kept looking at her watch. Her breathing had stepped up and her mouth was drawn down, stubborn and sullen. I was getting impatient.

"Why do you keep evading me?" I said. "I'm not trying to make trouble for you. Did you know that Barry Henley's wife was murdered the other night in a brutal, hideous way?"

She drummed with her fingers on a table top littered with Royal Copenhagen *objets d'art*.

"What's that to me?" she said with unexpected harshness. "I don't know these people."

Her voice had gone strident and I tried to keep my own under control.

"Why won't you talk to me? That's all I want."

"You mean you're lonesome?" she yelled. "Then go find somebody else to talk to!"

Without further warning she picked up one of the Danish pieces and flung it at my head. I ducked. It struck the wall and broke, crashing. I followed the impulse to look around. When I looked back a moment later she had opened a drawer in the table and brought a gun out of it. It was big and clumsy in her hand, but she could no doubt make it work all right and, as the club owner had told me, she was crazy.

"Get out of here," she said.

She came forward a few steps, holding the gun on me where I presented the best target. Where it would hurt the most.

"All right," I said, "but I think you're making a mistake."

She laughed with her mouth open. An ugly sound.

"You're the one making the mistake," she said. "I'm doing you a real favor. Don't you know whose house this is?"

I let her tell me.

"It's Brophy's. This is Brophy's house!"

"All right," I said.

I backed up to the door and found the knob with my left hand, watching her. She held the gun very steady.

"There's something else you might like to know," she said. "I'm Mrs. Brophy. I married Mr. Brophy a year ago in Las Vegas. We had a ball in Vegas. That's where I was when your private eye was looking for me. Does that clear things up for you?"

"Yes, ma'am," I said, opening the door. I slid outside and looked back. "I hope you have a long, happy life with Mr. Brophy."

I closed the door quickly because she was throwing the gun at me. It struck the door inside and I heard it drop to the floor with a thud. I went down off the porch and up the quiet street to my car. There was something cozy and homelike about it, especially the fragrance of the coffee I had spilled out of the paper containers.

CHAPTER THIRTEEN

A man runs out of drive. I had switched the phone to answering service but, as you know, even with that system, you still get the first two or three rings on your own gadget. At around noon on Sunday these began getting through to me. I tried to ignore it, but somebody was hot to talk to me. The thing would ring three times, click off, be quiet for one minute, then again three times. A concerted campaign. After half an hour of it, I gave in.

A male voice.

"You're in trouble," it said.

"The hell with it."

"You know how long it takes a man in concrete boots to get to the bottom of Lake Michigan?"

"Oh, knock it off," I said. "It's Sunday—"

"Stay away from Mrs. Brophy—every day, all day—at home, the club or on the street. Hands off."

He hung up.

I felt lousy. Trouble is for after breakfast. I dressed and went over to Tony's, which was pretty well filled with the Sunday hang-over crowd. The chatter was a pleasant blend of dirge and hilarity. Tony's "girls" were serving up their best macabre suggestions with gusto and leering delight. The one who took my order leaned close and spoke behind her hand.

"How about a Bloody Mary? Special today. Thirty dollars a pint—"

"On the side, huh?" I said. "With coffee."

She waggled her fanny at me, going away.

This sort of thing—I mean in general, not just the fanny waggling—has been going on at Tony's for at least fifteen years to my knowledge, but I understand it started back in the thirties, when whisky was ten cents a shot and the beer chaser came free.

I tried reading the paper, but the house copy was so messed up I couldn't make any continuity out of it. I ate breakfast at a leisurely pace and with accumulating relish. Somebody started the jukebox and I hung around awhile in spite of it, not admitting the hope that Bonny Thompson, my redheaded nurse, would drop in. But she didn't and I decided that maybe she went to church on Sunday and spent the rest of the day in meditation. It wasn't a gloomy picture. She was a girl who could do no wrong. She didn't know how yet.

When I stepped outside there was a long, new-looking Cadillac parked in front of the office across the street. I stood on the corner, fussing at my mouth with a toothpick, until the two guys sitting in it had moved around some. They turned out to be Paul Budge and his associate, Salford. So I went on across.

They came in and I offered them something and they turned it down. Unlike my neighborhood pals, they were not equipped with hangovers, but Budge looked as if he had been up all night, worrying. He probably worried quite a lot. I estimated that the Cadillac would wipe out about a third of his annual income, but that he was in that bad middle place where you had to spend money to make it and you couldn't ever make quite enough. Budge was by no means alone in this rat race but he was pretty typical of it. Salford was young and would bounce back pretty well, even if he had been drunk the night before, which I doubted. I had him figured for a worker.

"This is a pleasant surprise," I said. "What's up?"

Safford started to speak up, then deferred to Budge, as was proper.

"We had a strange experience last night," he said, working his hands. "Thought you ought to know about it. Understand you're co-operating with the police in this investigation about Virgie Henley."

"I guess you could say that."

"How is it going?" he asked.

I shrugged.

"We've turned over a lot of rocks, but not much turned up. It's a dry season."

"Yes," he said. "Well—around midnight last night a call came from a Miss Brenda Lundquist in Riverwood. Eric was in the office—"

I raised my eyebrows.

"Midnight Saturday and you were still in the office?"

Safford grinned a little shyly.

"I spend most of my nights there," he said. "Doing homework for one thing, trying to catch up."

"Go ahead," I said to Budge.

"This Miss Lundquist is employed by the Stanhope family, or what's left of it—"

"I know," I said. "What did Miss Lundquist want?"

"Eric said her conversation wasn't too coherent, but he gathered she was desperate about something. She insisted she had to see an attorney right away. Somehow she remembered my name from her brief association with Barry Henley."

"At midnight she had to see a lawyer?"

"Well, I was out of the office yesterday and so was Eric, until evening. I got the impression she had been trying to get me most of yesterday and didn't succeed until that hour. Naturally, Eric tried to put her off until Monday, but she wouldn't hear of it. He called me and we talked it over and decided to drive out to Riverwood and see her. If it hadn't been concerned with the Stanhope name and this Henley case I wouldn't have—"

"I understand," I said.

"We got out there at about one o'clock and it was Miss Lundquist who let us in."

"Was Miss Stanhope there?" I asked.

"Yes, she was reading. We met her, but she didn't enter into anything with us. In fact, Miss Lundquist pretty much hustled us into her own parlor upstairs. I got the impression that Miss Stanhope left the house a little later. Or maybe she went to bed.

"Anyway, Miss Lundquist launched on what seemed at first to be an utterly fantastic story, to this effect: That there is a plot against Miss Stanhope in the matter of her inheritance; that there has been fabricated a spurious will, purporting to contain Mr. Stanhope's last true testament, and that it is to be thrown into court at the last minute to delay and confuse the issue and open the whole matter to contest."

I stalled for time, offered them a drink and, when they turned it down again, poured a small one for myself and drank it.

"Who is supposed to be behind this plot?" I asked carefully.

"It's unbelievable," Budge said, "but this is what Miss Lundquist claimed: the notorious racketeer, Brophy, and—you."

"Me?"

"She said you are hounding her about it, distorting her words and prying into the Stanhope family affairs."

"Oh? On Brophy's behalf? Did she say I was working for Brophy?"

"Not in so many words."

"About this so-called will, did she say what it provided?"

"Only that it was an attempt to cut Dorothy Stanhope out of her inheritance."

I pawed it over mentally while I scratched my neck. I felt uncomfortable about it. Part of it could be made to fit all right, now that I knew Sister Carolyn was Mrs. Brophy. It gave Brophy a hell of a strong motive for marrying her. If the original will could be broken, there was a lot of money at stake; Carolyn could turn out to be worth a cool million.

I didn't like the last-minute feature. A plot like this ought to have been shaping up long before. At least as long before as—

Shortly following Barry Henley's death?

They were waiting for me to say something. There was one obvious thing to be said.

"How come you're telling me about it?"

"For one thing," Budge said, "I thought it was only fair to let you know about it. I'm sure in my own mind you're not working for Brophy. I told Miss Lundquist the same thing. I don't know whether she accepted it or not. For another thing, if there should happen to be a real, valid will that supersedes the will now in probate—well, all I can say is, somebody, somewhere, is going to need an attorney and maybe soon."

"Why?" I said.

He looked a little startled, as if it ought to be self-evident, as I guess it was.

"Well, if somebody has been suppressing it deliberately, that's a risky business."

"Only if it's found out," I said.

"Naturally."

Privately I was having a bad time. Barry Henley, I was thinking, not wanting to think it. "A black Irish bum," he had called himself. Leave the Irish out of it. A youngster beating his way up in a tough profession. I suppose it had been implicit in my theory from the start, but I hadn't let it out in the open. Virgie had helped me suppress it. The thought, that is, not the will, if any; though I thought surely there had to be one.

"If such a will exists," I said, thinking aloud then, "and if its effect would be to disinherit Dorothy Stanhope, then she would be the most interested party."

"Yes," Budge said, "but according to Miss Lundquist, Miss Stanhope has only the most blissful ignorance of any such idea."

"Miss Lundquist is a very loyal person," I said.

"So we gathered," Safford put in.

I wanted to be alone to think things over.

"I may want to ask you for some advice," I said, "professionally. But I'd like to wait awhile, anyway a few hours. Right now I might ask the wrong questions. Okay?"

"Please don't think I was making a pitch," Budge said. "That remark about somebody needing an attorney was just a figure of speech. I just wanted to fill you in."

"Understood," I said. "I appreciate it."

I got up and they followed the lead.

"I'll keep in touch," I said. "Did the police pick up those files yet?"

"Yesterday afternoon," Budge said. "I was sort of relieved to get rid of them."

"Uh-huh."

We went outside. The sun had come out and though it was still cold, there was a hint of spring in promise. The lazy Sunday street was empty. Faintly I could hear them balling it up over at Tony's.

I admired the Cadillac. Budge made a wry face.

"It looks great," he said. "But don't let it fool you. I spend a third of my time working to pay for it." I nodded sympathetically. I walked down there with them and Budge climbed in under the wheel, then Safford next to him. Budge tromped on the starter and nothing happened. He and Safford looked at each other and then at me. Budge was disgusted. I refrained from leering. He tried the starter some more. Nothing. Safford opened the door.

"That's another great feature," Budge said sourly. "Half the time it won't start."

"Come on in and have a drink and I'll call the Auto Club," I said.

Safford brushed past me.

"It's just the damn carburetor," he said. "I can fix it in a second. Nuisance, though."

The hood sprang open and Safford leaned over the motor. I stood around, not wanting to walk away from them, but not being any help either. Down the street a door sounded. I looked around and Bonny Thompson in her nurse's uniform was coming down the steps. I waved. She waved back and then stopped on the steps, looking my way. I cursed the fate that held me courteously with my guests. I was about to say goodbye anyway when the Cadillac motor came to life. Safford straightened, stuck a screwdriver in his hip pocket as if he had done it all his life, and got in with Budge. They waved and pulled away. I started down toward Bonny and she was pausing at the foot of her steps. Suddenly she turned her back on me and went away toward the hospital, quick and determined. There were footsteps behind me. I turned around and there was Donovan. Good old Donovan, my friend, my good, true, lucky, coincidental friend, on a quiet Sunday afternoon, and Bonny running away down the street.

She's got to get over being afraid of cops, I thought.

"I break something up?" Donovan said.

"Could be," I said. "Now you're here, come on in and have a cup of coffee."

Inside I happened to remember that he had been on foot. No car in sight anywhere.

"Just out for a Sunday stroll?" I asked.

"I took the bus. I'm on the run."

"That psycho after you?"

"Somebody. It must be him. I found a note from him when I got home last night. Crazy bastard."

"Glad you dropped in. He can get the both of us with his one rock."

"I knew you'd want to help. How come you haven't filed any reports the last few hours?"

I didn't bother with that.

"I'm just fine," I said. "How are your happiness boys?"

"Busy. We turned up plenty. We got about thirty, forty dynamite samples, a bunch of wire; we checked out eight or nine million mechanics; talked to everybody in that apartment where the Henley woman lived. We even shook down Whisky Davis a little."

"What did you get?"

"We didn't even get the time of day."

We sat over the coffee.

"I've got another question for you," I said.

"You're full of 'em, ain't you?"

"You're a sick old man, about to die. You've got a couple of daughters to provide for. No great problem there, you've got a couple of million you've saved up over a period of time. Only, it's not quite so simple. One of the girls is a good, solid, home-loving kid and that's all right. But the other one is on the wild side. In fact she ran away from home at an early age and you don't even see her.

"Still, you figure you can handle that, too. If you leave everything to the one daughter, the good one, you can figure she will see that the other one is taken care of. But then you learn something that rocks you back. Not only is the wild one a runaway, even a tramp, but she has fallen in with some scum; she is real thick with the scum. These are people who will take advantage of her—and, unavoidably, take advantage of the good daughter too. You get a picture of everything you worked for going down a dismal drain; to nobody; to scum."

I paused.

"All right, I got the picture," he said.

"What do you do about it?"

"You mean after I get hold of the tramp and take a strap to her?"

"You can't do that. She's of age and she's married. To this scum I mentioned."

I had his interest.

"Come again," he said.

"Carolyn Stanhope is married to Brophy."

"Well now."

He took off his hat and laid it on my desk.

"I think Barry Henley found out about the marriage and told the old man. I think the old man thought it over in a hurry and made a new will. I think this is what we're looking for."

"How much scratch did the old man leave?"

I told him.

"Brophy would be interested in that," he said.

While he thought about it, I did some pondering of my own, sudden and new in my mind. Brophy wasn't the only one. Foster Hayes might be interested too. Even in his position, it wouldn't do any harm to marry two million dollars. Then with Hayes and Brophy in a tug of war—

But that was going too fast.

Donovan looked at his watch and picked up his hat.

"Why don't you pull Brophy in?" I said.

"What for?"

"Well, it would make things a little more convenient for me."

He got up and stretched lazily. I could see the outline of that flat little automatic in his jacket pocket.

"I'll do that," he said. "I'll pick up Brophy and take him downtown. 'This bird-dog friend of mine,' I'll tell him, 'says that you married a Stanhope girl for her money and knocked off a couple of people so they wouldn't louse it up for you. Now you tell me all about it.' And while I'm talkin' to him like that, here comes a sharp, high-priced legal brain with a writ in his sticky fist and says, 'You can't talk to Mr. Brophy like that. What proof have you got?' And I'll say to him, 'Proof? You got to have proof? I just know. How do I know? Because there's this bird come down and set on my shoulder and told me, Brophy is the one.' And so then he says to me—"

"All right," I said. "Forget it. It was a nice dreamy thought at the time I had it."

"Don't get me wrong," he said. "I'd like to get Brophy. You find me a little evidence of some kind, like a receipt for a case of dynamite—"

"Yeah. Which way are you going?"

"I thought I would walk down and take a look at the lake. I lived in this town all my life and on Sundays and I been down to the beach about four times."

"There's nothing on the beach today. It's not even spring yet."

"There's enough. I can't stand that summer scenery any more at my age."

I picked up my hat and we went out. The sunshine had been modified by some dirty gray clouds and that cold breeze had sprung up. We walked down the street toward the lake, down hospital row, as it has come to be called. I thought about my bonny lassie with her dish full of thermometers and her little white cap. It was nice thinking about her. The hell with the Stanhopes and the Lundquists and the Brophy scum and that lousy jazz.

A block down the street, on the other side, they were razing one of the last of the old buildings in that neighborhood. They had thrown up a high board fence along the sidewalk, with peepholes at various levels. Of course, despite the peepholes, some eager sidewalk superintendents had managed to knock out a couple of boards here and there. I was pointing it out to Donovan and saying something about the new thing they were going to put up, and it was right along in there that we spotted the psycho.

He had evidently been standing in an areaway that adjoined the building site. When we made that point on our side of the street, he stepped out and started walking along with us, at our pace, all by himself, in a worn leather jacket too tight for him and a pair of ragged denim pants. I spotted him and knew him almost simultaneously, but I couldn't have told anybody how. When I glanced at Donovan, it was clear that he had spotted him too.

"Is he the one?" I asked.

"Yeah," Donovan said. "Just keep walkin'."

There was no place to hide. There weren't even any cars parked along this side of the street. We had a high brick wall on one side of us and the empty street and him on the other. Donovan cursed quietly under his breath. I was on the curb side of him, between them.

"Switch with me," he muttered.

"The hell with it. Maybe he'll pass it up on account of me."

"Do what I'm tellin' you!" he said through his teeth.

We switched places. The one across the street didn't break his stride, but he turned his body in an odd way and I could see the gun he was carrying in his right hand, down snug against his thigh. It was a big gun. I glanced at Donovan and his eyes were sweeping the street ahead for cover. There wasn't any between us and the next corner, an endless walk away.

The psycho stopped. I saw Donovan's hand slide into his pocket. I had a vivid, sickening picture of my own gun hanging on the bathroom door. A good safe place.

"Lieutenant!" the guy said.

He didn't have to shout. It was easy enough to hear.

"Donovan!" he said.

We stopped. Donovan half turned, very slowly.

"Remember me?" the guy said. "Remember what I said?"

"Don't do anything foolish," Donovan said. "There are two of us. You haven't got a chance."

He laughed. It was a frightening, sick laugh. I hope I never hear one like it again. He brought the gun up to his belt, holding it, not aimed yet.

"Sure I have, Donovan," he said.

Donovan's hand came up out of his pocket. The automatic would be in it. I had a couple of crazy impulses: like if I would make a break for a few paces, then double back quick and draw him off—or—but it was crazy thinking.

Shoot him, for God's sake! I thought.

Donovan's big frame knotted up. I could feel it. From heel to head, he drew himself into a taut trigger finger. That's all he was then for a few seconds, a gun with a man attached. I wanted to close my eyes, but couldn't. I couldn't even blink.

Sunday is a day off from school, a day to prowl the forbidden places, like vacant, unguarded building lots. This Sunday was the same as any other, except for the insane situation in which Donovan and his psycho and I found ourselves. In the same moment when Donovan turned himself into a shooting machine, three little boys came out through one of those holes in the fence.

They were aged about seven, eight and ten. I don't know whether they had been listening on the other side of the fence or not, but they came out through that hole in double time. When they caught sight of the man with the gun, they flattened against the fence like arrested puppets with their hands and feet in various impossible positions.

The smallest kid was nearest to the subject, about three feet away, and nobody on our side of the street was now going to do any shooting, unless it would be another psycho. Donovan had begun to shake slightly. Under his breath he called on heaven and hell simultaneously, with a tone of disbelief at the apparent decree that he was to die in helpless inactivity because of three kids he had never seen before in his long, dangerous, active life.

I was crying real tears of frustration and rage. The oldest of the kids, and farthest away from the psycho along the fence, was one I recognized from around the neighborhood—a tough, snotty kid. I hadn't been fond of him even under normal conditions.

"If I make a break for home," I said, "he'll swing with it, away from the kids and—"

"Nah," Donovan said. "They ain't got normal reflexes. And it's too close—if the kid should move—" He lifted his head and his voice: "Just put your gun down, son, and take it easy. No sense anybody gettin' hurt."

Again that laugh.

"Oh, no, Lieutenant—see—this gun is my friend—" He brought it up to where he could use it. I couldn't tell whether he knew the kids were there behind him. The little one edged off a few inches, hugging the fence with his shoulder blades.

Don't *move,* kid!

It could come at any moment now. It was a big gun and there wasn't much distance, maybe twenty yards. Donovan ground out words through his teeth.

"Keep your eye on him. I'm gonna dive for it. If he goes for me, you get those kids the hell out of there. Ready?"

"Ugh," I said.

He dived into the street and rolled awkwardly, twisting, toward the man with the gun. The psycho hunched forward excitedly, the gun dancing about, trying to focus on Donovan's erratically tumbling form. He started shooting. I stiff-armed the air.

"You kids—run!" I screamed.

The kids were frozen with fear or fascination. The psycho ran. He ran for the lake, right past the little peanut gallery, and the tough, snotty kid stuck his foot out and tripped him. I saw it plain because I was angling across the street after him and was only ten feet behind him when he went sprawling. The gun left his hand, slid across the walk and caromed off the board fence and beyond his reach. Just as I got to him he twisted, rolling, and I had to jump over him to avoid tripping myself. My shoulder used the fence for a cushion and I got hold of the gun. He was on his belly and hands, staring up at me with an open, frightened mouth. Donovan was on his knees in the middle of the street, his arm extended, his big hand not quite filled with the still useless and no longer needed automatic.

"Fellas," I said, watching the sick one on the walk, "move over here in back, huh?"

They filed past me, step by step, all eyes and hands and feet. I grinned stiffly at the biggest one.

"Nice going," I said. "Thanks."

He didn't say anything. I think he was getting scared by then.

"Let's get him the hell off the street," Donovan said, panting.

We had to lift and carry him through the narrow hole in the fence. On the other side, in the rubble of the leveled lot, he sat down against the fence with his arms around his raised knees and his head down on his knees. Donovan stayed with him while I went to put in the call.

Later, when we had washed up, we went over to Tony's and had a few— quite a few. The fracas down the street had become a rumor. Several people asked about it and I told them the naked facts briefly. It wasn't a thing to be described. If they had seen it—

But nobody had been watching.

CHAPTER FOURTEEN

The Stanhope mansion looked remote and austere in the cold, gray mid-morning. I had the eerie, never quite familiar feeling that all this had happened before. I wondered how it had looked to Barry Henley the first time he saw it. For one thing, it probably looked like the big strike, the doorway to glory and solvency.

I sat there in the street for a while, looking up between the big gates, wondering whether it was too early to go ringing the doorbell. A parcel delivery truck came up behind me, turned in and rolled up the drive to the house. I watched the man carry a couple of big packages to the door. He didn't have to wait long. Somebody came and took them. I couldn't tell whether it was Miss Lundquist or her mistress. The packages were Marshall Field type.

I followed the departing truck a little way down the quiet, tree-lined street, left my car at the curb and walked back up to the house by way of the curving drive. It was quite a hike. There were trees in the front yard and rose bushes and other shrubs on the sloping lawn. Except for a couple of pine trees, everything was dormant, the limbs of the trees black and skeletal looking. All the shades were drawn in the big house.

I pushed the bell, and after a couple of minutes Miss Stanhope opened the door. She was wearing a floor-length housecoat and boudoir slippers with pompoms on the toes. She was wearing her wonderful, skillful face, and her curly blond hair was neat and in place. But there were undisguised red rings around her eyes and I guessed that sometime in the last few hours, she had done some crying.

"Oh—it's you," she said.

"Yes. You promised to show me through the place."

"I did?"

"Yes, ma'am. The other day."

She held out for a few seconds, then smiled. It was a little one-sided, but not without grace, despite her reluctance.

"A promise is a promise," she said. "Please come in. I was just finishing breakfast."

She led me to the kitchen and I was glad to be second in line. There were the remains of a light breakfast on an enamel-top table and she took down a cup and saucer and poured me some coffee. She had the morning paper propped up on a silver sugar bowl. The coffee was very good.

"How are you coming with the investigation?" she asked.

"Not too good. I'd hoped you might tell me a little more about Carolyn."

She frowned a little and looked at her watch.

"I have an appointment downtown at one-thirty," she said. "If you want to make the tour of the old homestead, too—"

"All right. Maybe we could talk as we go."

She smiled suddenly, rather brilliantly. She was gorgeous when she smiled.

"What?" I said.

"Nothing," she said. "I imagine you're a very good detective."

"There's nobody I'd rather hear it from."

"Oh, come now," she said. "Ready?"

Then we were off on the tour and I got to follow her up the gigantic, spiraling staircase. She was chattering at me about who had built it and when, which, as I remembered, was not long after the Civil War. I was mumbling occasionally, something like, "They don't build them the way they used to."

On the balcony, I pointed up at the portraits. "Family ancestors?" I asked.

She laughed. "No, they came with the house. Father used to call them the 'Board of Directors.' He got sort of attached to them, I think."

"I can see that he might."

"They used to frighten Carolyn and me half to death. There was a certain hour, about sundown, when the light played tricks with their faces, you know?"

She shivered unexpectedly and gripped my arm. She actually seemed to be reliving it, the girlhood, the fear and the trembling.

I was having mental trouble over her. From her first haughty, standoffish, occasionally downright offensive attitude, she had switched, and with not much time in between.

Moody, I thought. Moody and mixed up.

And I thought, Why not? With all this establishment and nobody to have any fun with except Mr. Hayes and Brenda Lundquist.

"Miss Lundquist isn't here?" I said.

"No. She had to go out early today. She'll be back this afternoon."

She was leading me along the upstairs hall toward the rear of the house. At the end of the hall was a door and beyond it, no doubt, a balcony. There was always a balcony. There were pictures here, too, on the walls on both sides: old landscapes, ladies in ball gowns doing the minuet with gentlemen in lace cuffs. I could almost hear the violins.

The door opened with a squeak and a groan. Light came in shockingly and with it, fresh cold air. There was still the odor of winter in it.

From the balcony we looked out over the back lot of the estate. Some lot. It covered at least a full country acre. I calculated that the stand of timber at the far back was a hundred years old: oak and pine. There were a good many fruit trees and near the house a formal garden, precise and carefully trimmed.

"There's Carolyn's room," she said, pointing.

I guess I did a double take. She laughed.

"You'll see it," she said. "Just keep looking."

I finally found it; a sort of English cottage, almost hidden in a grove of trees off to our right. It took shape and I could make out the low-hanging eaves and the heavy oak door with big brass hinges. From where we stood it looked far away and unreal, like a toy house.

"Would you like to see it?" she asked.

"Sure," I said. "Do we go down the ivy here, or shall we take the stairs?"

She looked a little suspicious. I grinned at her and after a moment she returned it. We turned back into the upstairs hall. I followed her past the double row of closed doors.

"Which room did your father die in?" I asked.

She stopped and turned to me slowly.

"He died in the hospital," she said.

"Yes, but he had this rather long illness. Was he in the hospital all the time?"

"Oh—I see. That was his room." She pointed to one of the doors on our left. "In the last few weeks he never left it. Why did you ask?"

"What?"

"About his room? What difference does it make?"

"Nothing particular," I said. "I know that Henley had some meetings with him and I presumed they would have taken place wherever your father was at the time."

"Well, if you think it would be helpful to your investigation to see his room, you're welcome."

"Thank you."

She opened a door and stood back to let me in. It was a large airy room, thickly carpeted, with bookcases and masculine appointments, including mounted game trophies, an old golf bag, the clubs still carefully wrapped, some fishing tackle and a pipe rack on a bedside table. It looked comfortable and lived in, not especially died in.

"He led an active life," I said.

"Yes. He only took over during the war out of patriotism. He had been retired for a long time."

"That would have been back East?"

"Yes, in Boston."

We came to the stairs, in the shadow of the ancient commanders on the walls. She lifted the skirt of her robe to go down. Her feet were small and shapely in the slippers. Her back was straight, her shoulders feminine.

"Does the servant live in the house, or is there a separate building?" I asked.

She looked at me sharply.

"If you mean Miss Lundquist, I don't think of her as a servant."

"Excuse me."

"She has an apartment in that wing."

To my left the portrait gallery ended in a door that would lead into the east wing of the house. When I joined her for the descent, she was pouting a little. I tried to think of a pleasantry, but instead, all I could think of was of walking down an old, worn, familiar street of the city with Virgie Henley on my arm, tiny and scared, and the horrible sound of the explosion, and there was nothing funny to be said to this bright, rich, beautiful girl. Somebody else would have to lighten her dreary path through life.

She opened a closet under the staircase and took out my topcoat and a light wrap for herself.

"Will that be enough?" I asked, helping her into it. "It's a cold day."

"I'm very warm-blooded," she said.

She was still angry with me and I kept discreetly quiet as we went out through the pantry and kitchen and outside. The cold air struck harsh and clean at my face. Looking out across the vast lot, I could see, beyond the winter-black lacework of the garden, the low English cottage with its steep gable and the ivy crawling along the eaves.

Dorothy Stanhope walked rapidly, hugging herself with her arms, so that her stride was stiff and taut, peg-like. The ground under the garden path was concrete-hard. At the cottage door, she produced a key. The heavy panel swung creakily, opening inward. There was the odor of burned wood.

Except for the mirror, it was an ordinary, comfortable, den-like room, furnished with odds and ends, some antique, others modern. There was a modest hi-fi set with an open metal rack for records, mostly ten-inch. There were casual chairs and tables and a large couch opposite the hi-fi, piled with multicolored cushions. A door stood open beside a rustic fireplace, and beyond it I could see part of a bedroom and dressing room. The fireplace mantel was of stone. Above the mantel hung this mirror.

It must have been twelve feet square, an antique with a huge, ornate frame. It was hung with a slight forward tilt so that without craning my neck I could see practically all of the room in which we stood and both of us, full length. The glass was either tinted or of rare manufacture and gave a clear but rather dark image. Miss Stanhope's face was somewhat softened and grayed in reflection.

She looked up at herself for a few moments, then turned, almost with a dancing step, spread her arms and smiled.

"This is Carolyn's room," she said. "How do you like it?"

"Well, I'm not used to it yet."

"I think it's quite nice. I think Carolyn likes it too, but she doesn't show her feelings much."

Only anger, I thought.

"Does she come home often?" I asked.

"Only once in a while. We keep the room for her. Sometimes she'll come for a night or two, but she has an apartment in town somewhere."

"Do you know where?"

"No. I think she doesn't want any ties from us to her; just the other way she wants it, so she can come home if she wants to."

"Those are her records?"

"Yes. Some of them she made herself."

"How does she sing?"

"Like a dark angel, sweet and lowdown. Want to hear some? Here, let me start the fire."

She knelt on the hearth and struck a foot-long match, turned on a gas jet and set fire to the logs already laid. There was a considerable pile of accumulated ashes.

"Very cozy place," I said.

She smiled, setting the records on the changer.

"Isn't it?" she said. "We used to share it when we were girls. It was mysterious and scary."

The music started, low and torchy.

"When did she leave home for the first time?" I asked.

Dorothy crossed the room and sat back on the couch. She sat with crossed ankles drawn to one side and with her long and, as I remembered, lovely legs in prim conjunction. She found a cigarette someplace and I walked over to light it for her.

"When she was fifteen," she said, through a curl of smoke. "Kids go through a stage like that, even girls. It's more dangerous for girls than for boys, but Carolyn was lucky. She never got into real trouble."

"How long would she stay away?"

"Sometimes overnight, sometimes for two or three days."

"What about the school authorities?"

"She never ran away from school—that was one of the odd things about it. Just from home—from Father and, I suppose, me and—" she gestured toward the house—"that big barn of a place."

"You never knew where she went or what she did?"

"Not at first. Then little by little I began finding things—matchbooks, strange names jotted down on scraps of paper. Sometimes when she felt close to me, she would drop hints."

"Wasn't your father aware of this? Did he try to do anything about it?"

"He knew something about it, but I covered for her quite a lot. It wasn't till after I had gone away to school, when the whole responsibility fell on him, that he really began to worry about her. By then, of course, she was eighteen."

"Where did you go to school?"

"In the East, a small college for women. I think Carolyn might have left home long before, if I hadn't been here up till then. When I went away, I guess she just decided there wasn't much to stay home for."

Carolyn's voice was singing, low and torchy. It was the same voice all right. It seemed more effective than in the club, without the distraction of that peekaboo dress.

"Did Carolyn spend last night here?" I asked.

She looked faintly surprised.

"Not that I know of," she said, "and I usually know. She usually at least says hello."

"But it would be possible for her to come here and spend the night and you wouldn't notice?"

"Yes, depending on the time of night and whether she turned on lights or started the fire. You can't hear anything that goes on here, though, not from the house."

I was having a new experience in my trade. Nearly all people get edgy under questioning; they tend to freeze up after a certain length of time. But Dorothy Stanhope was loosening up. She was getting almost garrulous, as if she had nothing better in the world to do than to sit around and chat with me about her family problems. I felt a little giddy, as if I had the world by the tail and nobody to tell me when to let go.

The throbby beat of the music was getting under my skin. Miss Stanhope's left foot was beating in time, rocking the couch in rhythm. I took a turn around the room. She snuffed out her cigarette.

"It's a good beat," she said. "Would you like to dance?"

She came up gracefully in a continuous, smooth motion and I took her in my arms. She danced well and smoothly, a little reserved, not pressing close and, on the other hand, not standing back. It seemed simultaneously odd and natural that we should be dancing.

"Excuse me," I said.

"For what?"

"For doing all this talking about your sister. When there's you."

She laughed, warm against my neck.

"Part of your job, isn't it? All right to combine business with pleasure?"

"Any time."

More than the music was getting under my skin. Reserved or not, she was every inch a woman, felt like one, vibrated like one.

"How do you like Foster?" she asked me.

"Mr. Hayes?"

"Yes. I understand you had cocktails the other day."

"He told you?"

"Uh-huh." She gave that soft laugh again. "Good old Foster. He does try."

"Are you going to marry him?"

"Probably. But not today."

The beat had stepped up a little and she was closer. It was the old, old setup. The place, the time, the girl. I could feel it in my throat and in my temples and elsewhere. I knew it was crazy, that it would louse up everything I had left to do, and I knew I was going to try.

But I guess she knew it too, and a little bit sooner. The record came to an end. It was awfully quiet in the room, except for the firewood crackling. She moved out from me a little. Her fingers were interlaced at the back of my neck. There was a slight flush on her face and a crease of frown in her forehead. She put her head down for a moment against my chest.

"I'm sorry," she said. "I like you, Mac. I like you very much. But I do have an appointment. I have to get dressed."

"May I drive you downtown?"

"No, thanks. I'll have to have a way to get home and I'll be all afternoon—"

"I'll wait."

She looked up, smiling.

"I know you would, but you're a busy man. Please, let's stop now, huh?"

And that was what it came to. She walked ahead of me to the big house, holding her skirt up to keep it from dragging in the dirt. The cold air restored my equilibrium. More or less. At the front door, I held the edge of it for a moment and asked when I might see her again.

"I don't know," she said hurriedly. "You might call sometime."

"I just might."

She kissed me then, light and quick on the cheek. While she was doing it, my finger found the night latch and pushed. It didn't make a sound. She closed the door.

* * * *

I walked down the drive and down the street to my car and got in and sat there. Half an hour passed. A station wagon came out of the gate with Dorothy Stanhope at the wheel. She turned away from where I was parked, headed for the city. I let her get out of sight. Then I climbed out, walked back to the mansion and up the drive and let myself in by way of the unlocked door she hadn't bothered to check.

Miss Lundquist's rooms were immaculate and in perfect order. They were also sparsely furnished, with a minimum of knickknacks and gewgaws. It took me five and a half minutes to find what I was looking for, in the bottom drawer of a small desk, under a box of scented, monogrammed writing paper.

There were two copies, an original and a carbon. It read:

> This is the last will and testament of William V. Stanhope, sound in mind and body. It shall supersede any and all previous wills under my hand and seal.
>
> I direct my executors, the National Trust and Savings Bank of Chicago, to place in trust the cash residue of my estate, after payment of just debts and taxes; and to pay an income based on sound financial management from said trust to my daughter, Dorothy Stanhope. Under no circumstances shall the principal amount of said trust be paid in a lump sum to my daughter or to any other claimant.

It was signed "William V. Stanhope" in a firm hand, and dated March 3rd of the previous year. It had been witnessed by "Barry Henley" and "Brenda Lundquist."

I was checking the copy to make sure it was identical when the door opened and Brenda Lundquist came into the room.

CHAPTER FIFTEEN

I couldn't blame her for being upset. She didn't look like a bird any more, just like a distraught woman suffering from invasion of privacy and I didn't know what else. She put out a hand and found a place to support herself.

"You—" she said.

"Yes. I'm sorry you had to find me. I thought I could get out before you came back."

She looked at the papers in my hand.

"With those, I suppose," she said.

I folded the two legal-size sheets and laid them on a chiffonier. There was a photograph on it that I hadn't even noticed before: a small, oval portrait of two blond, curly-headed little girls, aged about three. Dorothy and Carolyn.

A little dazedly she wandered to a chintz-covered settee and put down her purse. She took off her gloves, pulling idly at the fingers.

"Want to talk to me about it?" I asked.

"There's nothing to talk about."

"What I don't understand," I said, "is why you kept them all this time. Why didn't you just destroy them as soon as Mr. Stanhope died?"

"You don't understand—"

"I know. That's what I'm saying."

Slowly she sank down on the settee and sat with her hands in her lap, the fingers moving idly, at random.

"Didn't Mr. Stanhope direct you to send these to the bank? After sending one copy along with Barry Henley, just for insurance?"

"No," she said. "Mr. Stanhope—wanted me to keep these. These were the insurance! They weren't to be used or disclosed unless something developed in the settlement of the original will. They were just in case any trouble developed."

"That's not the way it reads," I said. "It reads precisely as if he meant every word of it then and now."

Her mouth moved without sound. I wanted to believe her, but it was awfully hard to do.

"I'm not a lawyer," I said, "but I don't think you can write a legal will on that kind of contingency."

"It's true," she said stoutly.

"It could be," I said, "though I would think that Mr. Stanhope would have known better. If he didn't know himself he surely could have called his attorney or the bank—"

"There wasn't time!" she said. "He thought he was dying. It was Sunday—"

"Another reason for keeping a will like this around," I said, "is that it makes wonderful extortion material."

"What do you mean?"

"Well, you ask any ten people whether they would rather have two million in cash or the income from two million under conservative management, and nine of them will take the two million. So you could figure that it would be worth quite a lot to such a person to keep the existence of a document like this one a very deep secret. To Dorothy Stanhope, in this case, it might be worth half the estate."

"No! I would never do such a thing—"

"Maybe not. I don't know. I found these copies in your desk. I'm not too clear on why you would wait so long, until the estate was due to be settled under the original will at any moment. But of course, the tension mounts in the heir—or heiress—as the big money gets closer and closer. The emotional condition might be ripe for a touch at such a time whereas earlier—"

She came up off the settee and her hands were making futile little fists in my direction.

"I won't have you say such things! Get out!"

"In just a minute. Was it Brophy Mr. Stanhope was worried about? Did he find out that Carolyn was Brophy's wife?"

"He left the estate to Dorothy!"

"I know, but there are all sorts of ways and means and a man like Brophy doesn't go by the rules."

Her face was flushed and her breathing extremely agitated. I did not want her to have a heart attack, especially not in my lone presence.

"Let's forget it for now," I said. "Does Dorothy know about this will?"

"Naturally not."

"Why naturally?"

"She's a thoroughly honest woman."

I turned to the chiffonier. I picked up the folded documents and turned them a few times in my hand. I looked at the photograph of the two little girls and then at Miss Lundquist again.

"What are you going to do?" she asked quietly. "Are you going to take them? Turn them over to the court?"

"No," I said. "It's not really my concern." I put the sheets back on the chiffonier. "I would make this suggestion though; that you either destroy them now, right away, and forget you ever saw them; or show them to Dorothy Stanhope and talk it over with her. I have no conscience in this. Money is only money. It is never anything else. I would hate to see Brophy come into any of Mr. Stanhope's money, but if that's the risk you and Miss Stanhope want to run—" I walked over to the door. On a small stand near it was a silver tray with a single white business card lying on it face down. I picked it up and turned it over. It read: "Paul Budge, Attorney at Law."

"You didn't tell Mr. Budge about this will when he was here the other night?" I asked.

"No. I was consulting Mr. Budge about another matter."

"I see."

I dropped the card onto the tray.

"All right, Miss Lundquist, I guess it's up to you. You and Miss Stanhope. Two heads are better than one."

And all that jazz, I thought as I let myself out.

I drove to the Loop and had lunch and then I went over to headquarters and looked up Sergeant Monday.

"A few months back," I said, "some guy in the restaurant business got a working over from Brophy's boys."

He scratched his head and thought back.

"Yeah," he said. "On the South Side."

"I mean the one that declined to testify after."

"I know who you mean."

"You have any pictures of him?"

He blinked at me.

"That's not my department—"

"Well, could you look them up for me? Just two or three of them."

"I don't know—"

"No hurry. If you have to clear it."

"I sure as hell would have to clear it with somebody."

"I want to take them out."

"Oh, Mac—"

"It's important," I said, "or I wouldn't ask."

"Sure, but you know how it is."

"I know how it is. Maybe Donovan could help."

"I'd have to do a lot of checking around."

"I got the time," I said.

He shifted uneasily and fussed with his shirt and tie and coughed a little and picked up a phone and put it down again.

"If you don't mind?" he said, pointing to the waiting room outside.

"Sure," I said. "I'll be there."

"Yeah," he said.

I went out and sat on a hard bench and read the morning paper three times from cover to cover. Then I sat and stared at the floor. At about three o'clock, two hours after my arrival, Sergeant Monday came out with a manila envelope in his hand.

"It better be important," he said.

"It's important. Thanks. Buy you a drink one of these days?"

"Okay, Mac."

He went away. I took my pictures home, undressed and took a shower and changed clothes. It was almost five when I was dressed and I made a small drink and sat over it, waiting and waiting. There was some chance I could wait out the rest of my life. It was like one roll of the dice for double or nothing with the rules subject to change without notice at the discretion of the dealer.

I waited till eight o'clock and then hung a note on the door and went over to Tony's to get something to eat. I had no more than taken the first bite when Dorothy Stanhope came in looking for me.

CHAPTER SIXTEEN

I was toward the back and had a chance to look her over before she found me. I was pleased to note that her lip didn't curl, nor did her patrician nose levitate. She was wearing all her dignity, but without playing little Miss Gotrocks. Tony's girls worked her over ruthlessly with their eyes, but it didn't cause her any noticeable discomfort. She passed the "Tony" test pretty well.

When she spotted me in the back booth, her head went up a notch and she came on quickly. I stood up and she slid in across from me. I lit her cigarette for her and she inhaled and blew a couple of rings and settled back, smiling that odd half-smile.

"What am I going to do about you?" she said.

One of the girls drifted suggestively toward the booth, giving her that female once-over again.

"Hungry?" I asked. "This is sandwich night at Tony's. What kind of salami sandwich would you like?"

Oh, come on, old-timer, I thought.

She laughed politely and looked up at the waitress.

"Scotch and water, please," she said.

She was quite gracious about it. I was getting proud of her. Of course, we had a long way still to go.

"It wasn't friendly of you to search Brenda's room," she scolded.

I looked at her and she wasn't exactly kidding, but she wasn't too outraged either.

"I guess not," I said, "but on the other hand, I may have done both of you a service."

"I'm trying to think so. What possessed you to do it?"

"That's easy. I wanted to find that will and I had a tip as to where it might be hidden."

"Not hidden," she said. "Just kept in a safe place."

"As you wish," I said.

She ran the gloved tip of her right forefinger along the edge of the table.

"What I was going to do," she said, "when the estate could be settled—I was going to make some investments of my own."

"I understand," I said.

Some time went by while she worked slowly at her drink.

"Brenda said you mentioned someone named Brophy," she said, "in connection with Carolyn."

I signaled the waitress and paid the tab.

"Yes," I said. "Carolyn, it turns out, is married to Brophy. You know about Brophy, of course."

She shook her head stiffly.

"No."

I got up and gave her a hand.

"Let's go over to the office and talk about it."

She came along all right, clear across the street and into my open doorway. There she hung herself up for a minute.

"It's a little more than just an office, isn't it?" she said.

"Whatever you want to make it," I said.

She came in then. I arranged seating accommodations and set an ash try within her reach, a big ash tray. She took off her gloves and coat. She was wearing a gray dress of a soft material, similar to the one she had been wearing that first day I saw her.

"This morning—" she said, "you didn't tell me you had talked with Carolyn."

"No, ma'am. I was building up to it when we started dancing. Then it kind of slipped my mind."

"I see."

I made her a drink and did some stalling. Every few minutes I would feel her like a needle under the skin and I had to shake it off and get objective again. It wasn't always easy.

"You take things very calmly," I said, "considering your age and situation."

"I don't think age has much to do with it, do you?"

"Sometimes. Did you know Carolyn was Brophy's wife?"

"Yes," she said quietly, "I knew."

"And that's all? 'Yes, I knew'?"

"What else?" she said. "Carolyn is of age; it's a free country."

"It wouldn't be a free country if there were many more like Brophy. And things are tough enough as it is."

"What do you mean?" she said.

"Brophy is a criminal," I said.

"By whose lights?"

It was exasperating. I kicked myself back from the desk and made a drink for myself. Then I decided not to drink it. She was sitting calmly in her chair, watching me all the time and I found I couldn't look at her and talk to her at the same time. I talked to the wall.

"Brophy—I'll tell you about Brophy. He is a set of brass knuckles. He is the reinforced toe of a steel boot. He is what they mop up off the floors of restrooms after people have been sick in them."

"Oh really—" she said.

"If the best of our civilization is based on the dignity of individual human beings, then Brophy is a Cro-Magnon type. Look, I'm an ordinary little guy with some money to invest, and I decide to go into the restaurant business, open a small club. I find out everything costs more than I figured—supplies, furnishings, equipment; I have to arrange terms. Somebody tells me, 'Go see Brophy. He'll fix you up.'

"I see Brophy. He works everything out. It's a breeze. He's got everything I need, he'll finance it for six percent—plus a percentage of the take, every Saturday night at closing time. Every Saturday night. But I don't know this till after the deal is closed and the stuff is in. Too late then. I got everything of my own in it. I have to run the club or start over from scratch, from nothing!

"So every Saturday night there's a guy from Brophy sitting around till I close and then we go through the register together and he counts out Brophy's cut. I get fed up with this. I want to rewrite the deal. I go to a bank. The bank hears about Brophy and I can't raise a lead slug. I protest to Brophy. The next Saturday night I refuse to let the guy take the cut out of the register. He warns me, but I'm desperate and I throw him the hell out.

"The next night, Sunday, they work over my joint. All the bottles from the bar are broken and the place smells like an old beer vat. The carpets are ruined and the upholstery slashed. All the glasses are smashed and the pieces scattered all over the place. I've got nothing in the world but this wreckage and I have to buy ten thousand dollars' worth of new stuff. Where can I get it? One guess, honey. From Brophy!

"I go to the cops. They're glad to see me. They show me pictures. Maybe one of them is the guy who was coming around for the Saturday night cut. I say, 'Yeah, that's him.' When I come out of the police house, a couple of guys are waiting for me. We go for a little ride to some quiet, deserted place. And these two guys explain to me what a mistake I made. They don't use any words; just their hands and feet."

I took some of my drink. She was sitting very rigid in the chair. Her cigarette was down to her fingers, but she wasn't smoking it. Otherwise, she wasn't reacting. I had to get a reaction out of her. I grabbed the envelope Sergeant Monday had given me, tore it open and yanked out the photographs. One by one I tossed them in her lap, with plenty of time in between.

"That's me after they get through with the explanation," I said. "That thing hanging down my face that looks like a grape—that's my left eye!"

She covered her eyes with her hand. The cigarette burned her fingers and she dropped it. I stepped on it. I picked up the photographs and stuffed them down in the wastebasket.

"That's Brophy," I said. "That's Carolyn's husband, that figures he can get a million bucks, maybe two million, out of the Stanhope estate. One way or the other."

"No—!" she gurgled.

"Yes. But a big fat yes! That's the guy who is paying off the owner of the 401 Club every Saturday night to keep Carolyn on as an entertainer, because she couldn't ever make it on her own talent."

You never can be sure what will get to somebody. When I told her Brophy was paying Carolyn's way, she looked at me and there was horror in her face.

"No—" It was more a whimper than a protest.

"Yes. It sounds like a switch, huh? Brophy paying somebody off? But what the hell—look at the stakes."

She came up unsteadily and I had to support her for a moment till she got her balance. She had her gloves in one hand and her purse in the other and was gesturing with them in a vague, lost way. I took her arm, none too gently.

"Come on, I'll show you how it works down there where Brophy and his boys live."

She hung back.

"Mac, please—"

"Come on!" I said. "Nobody will make trouble for you. You're the golden goose, baby."

She came along, still hanging back, but making no scene. Her station wagon was parked in front of my car at the curb. There was a parking ticket slipped under her windshield wiper. I pulled it loose and stuck it in my pocket.

She got in readily enough when I opened the door, and sat in a huddle against the door. I got under the wheel. We didn't have any conversation during the short trip. For myself, I decided I had done enough talking and I don't know what Miss Stanhope was thinking; nor have I been able to make a reasonable guess since.

* * * *

If the 401 Club had died on Saturday night, it was being embalmed on Monday. The piano player was picking at his instrument in a lackadaisical way; the bartender was picking his idle teeth and there was only one waitress on duty. There were only the three of them in the room when Dorothy and I went in.

She had made one feeble protest against going in, but hadn't really put up a fight. When she saw how empty the joint was, she moved with more alacrity. Going ahead of me, she selected an out-of-the-way table for two. The lights were very dim and I knew the bartender couldn't have recognized us. The waitress, however, came closer and did a take when she saw Dorothy. But she recovered in a hurry, as waitresses do. We ordered Scotch and water.

"So this is it," Miss Stanhope said, glancing around. "This is where she sings."

"Uh-huh," I said.

Over the drinks, she looked around some more.

"I don't get any impression such as the one you were trying to give me," she said.

"It's early," I said.

"It's after eleven."

"That's early."

"Just what do you expect to happen?" she asked.

"I don't know."

With a little sigh she settled down with her drink. I was sorry to be grumpy, but I was on a painfully sharp edge. I thought I knew pretty well what to expect, but there was a chance that nothing at all would happen. Something would have to happen, just a little something, almost anything, but something.

We discussed the decor. Dorothy's taste ran along different lines. So did mine, but the hell with it.

We discussed the weather and that didn't take long. The waitress came with a new round of drinks and we nursed them and looked at each other and away from each other and there was a band of sweat around my neck like fine lace.

Then finally it began to happen. I noticed the owner in his tuxedo sitting at the bar. I saw the waitress talking to him. When she moved aside, I saw him look in our direction and hold it. He held it for a long time by my count. Then he got on his feet and came our way. The piano player launched himself on a fortissimo rendition of "Begin the Beguine."

The guy reached the table and smiled with all the benevolence of a hyena over a piece of carrion.

"Having a pleasant evening?" he asked.

Dorothy looked up and smiled graciously.

"Very nice, thank you," she said.

"How are you tonight?" he asked me.

"Just fine," I said. "We came to listen to Miss Stanley. I told my friend about her—"

"Miss Stanley won't be on tonight; I'm sorry," he said.

"Oh?" I said.

"She doesn't work Monday nights."

"How disappointing," Dorothy said.

He looked at her. The knuckles of his clenched fist on the table were white.

"I wonder if I could have a word with you?" he said to me.

"Well—"

"You may be excused," Dorothy said, "but hurry back."

I got up slowly. The guy in the tux was walking toward the bar. I followed him halfway along, then stopped. After a moment he looked back, hesitated and returned to me. I shifted my feet and I could see our table in one direction and enough of him in the other.

"This is far enough," I said. "What?"

He came to the point.

"You take that woman and get the hell out of here," he said, "now. Right now. Just blow."

"Look, I—"

He looked at his watch.

"I'll give you time to finish your drinks, if you don't waste any time. Then get out. I mean it."

I gazed around the room.

"Seems to me you can use the business," I said.

"Never mind about the business. Just blow."

"Can't we talk it over—?"

"We did that already. Now you get back there and drink up and take your lady and I mean go!"

I shrugged and went back to the table.

"What was it?" she asked.

"Nothing special. He apologized for the lack of entertainment and said he planned to close up in about five minutes, so if we want another drink we better order it now. How about you?"

"No, thanks."

"Then we'll see if we can't find a livelier spot."

"We'll see little Dorothy home, if you don't mind," she said.

"The night is young—"

"Please, Mac."

I was getting it from all sides. I drank up and waved in a friendly way at the owner, seated now at the bar. There was no response. I was helping Dorothy into her coat when the front door opened and Brophy came in with Whisky Davis. A moment later Mr. America slipped in and stood in the little foyer with his arms folded. Brophy and Davis walked down the center to the bar and I saw the owner get up uncertainly and look around and sit down again. If Brophy or Davis saw Dorothy and me, they didn't let it rock them.

"Oh, God," Dorothy said suddenly, hoarse and low in her throat, "get me out of here."

"Sure," I said, "but don't be worried. You've got the power—"

"Just get me out!" she said through her teeth.

"Okay," I said, "the side door."

The red exit sign was off to our left. The blind alley ran down to it off Rush Street, I remembered.

I took her arm and we started over there. The fire door opened and a guy stepped inside—Brophy had brought the whole corps tonight. It was a business call and we were in the middle. It was possible we were the cause of it.

Dorothy wrenched free, twisted away from me and ran for the front door. I chased her. She was nearly in the foyer when Mr. America unfolded his arms. Then he caught sight of me coming on, stepped aside and Dorothy pushed through the door and out. There was more light up here. I could see the look on his face. It was a look of eager anticipation.

All I had on him was momentum. In flight, I picked up a chair made of heavy aluminum tubing and plastic and swung all the way around with it. I missed him. The swing had carried me against the black plastic quilted wall of the foyer and he jumped over the chair and was on me. He hit me once in the face and once in the chest and I slid down on his feet. It had been a high blow and glancing, so I had the one more chance. I wrapped my arms around his knees and pulled up and he dumped backward. I was still on my own knees when I got hold of the door and I didn't get straight till I had overrun the curb outside and was halfway across the street. I hadn't quite made it in time. Dorothy Stanhope's station wagon was disappearing down the avenue. I watched it turn left at Chicago, heading for home.

Somebody shouted and I ducked and ran on to the other side of Rush Street. When I looked around, I saw it had not been Mr. America or any of those others. The street was relatively well lighted and patrolled. It was no place for a brawl.

I walked two blocks, found a taxi and got to the office. It was about a quarter to twelve. I checked on the damage from the fracas and it didn't amount to much. I went back out to the car, got it warmed up and made for Riverwood.

CHAPTER SEVENTEEN

I didn't bother with the main house, but left the car on the drive and made for the cottage by a tree-lined path, past the winter-black shadows of shrubs alongside the house and then the dormant formal garden. I could see the cottage was lighted. A soft glow of light edged the heavy front door with its ornate brass hinges.

It had been pushed to but was not quite on the latch. I caught my breath, opened the door silently and went in. She was standing in the middle of the room, looking up into the great mirror. She was quite motionless, her hands at her sides, peering up at herself and I could see what I ought to have seen long before: that odd double image, the grown-up remnant of the old portrait in Brenda Lundquist's room, of the two little twin girls with the curly blond hair.

Her eyes shifted slowly, as if by painful effort, and by way of the mirror she looked at me.

"So you know now?" she said.

"I guess so. Barry Henley got this far, too, didn't he?"

"Yes."

She squared her shoulders and lifted her head. There was a smudge of lipstick at one corner of her mouth and she tried to rub it out with her finger, but only made it worse. Her shoulders slumped again. She dropped her head forward and the palms of her hands turned helplessly to the mirror.

"Mac—help me!"

"I'll listen," I said. "How did Carolyn die?"

It took her a while to get it up. When it started, she talked straight to the mirror, as if she were telling it to someone she could see up there. Maybe she could.

"We were four years old. In the summers we used to go to an old farm in Vermont. We loved it. Our mother was ill then, but we didn't know it. She smiled a lot and was very sweet to us, though she must have been suffering badly.

"A middle-aged couple named Peter and Melody took care of the farm, and us, too, and my mother had a nurse-companion, Aunt Hattie. She was kind of grumpy and didn't have much to do with us. Peter and Melody took good care of us, but they had other things to do, too, so we were on our own quite a lot.

"About half a mile from the house there was an old stone quarry. We weren't allowed to go there. It was a strict rule and we knew it. I can't account for what happened this particular day, except that everyone must have been busy; and maybe Peter was away in town that day. Anyway, Carolyn and I wandered away from the house and pretty soon we were headed for the forbidden stone quarry as fast as we could go. As usual, I was in front. Carolyn was the cautious one, but she would go wherever I went—mostly.

"At first it was enough of a thrill that we were in the vicinity of the quarry. The idea of doing anything about it didn't occur to us. We played around the woodlot, picking flowers and turning over stones and things. After a while we got bored—or I did—and began edging closer to the quarry.

"It was a deep pit with water at the bottom. There had been a wooden fence around the rim, but it had fallen apart and the rails were scattered all over the place. I remember that where we played in the wood-lot was quite a distance from the rim.

"I was fascinated by it, but frightened too. I wanted to go over there, but not alone, and I was afraid that if I came right out with it, Carolyn would refuse. So I—I *maneuvered* her into it!"

She put her hands to her face and I saw she was trembling.

"Steady," I said.

She made herself go on.

"I maneuvered in such a way that pretty soon we were both right on the rim. When Carolyn realized it, she wanted to leave right away. I wouldn't let her. I wanted to see. I was afraid to walk right to the edge, so I lay down on my stomach and kind of inched up to it. It was awfully scary. It looked a thousand feet deep. All down the sides were jagged rocks. The water in the bottom was like dirty, gray glass, dead looking.

"Carolyn started to cry. I told her to shut up and that only made her cry harder. She begged me to come away from the edge and go home with her. She took hold of one of my ankles and started pulling on it. I got furious, and the next thing I knew we were fighting, hitting and clawing at each other, and Carolyn was crying and I lost my temper. I didn't realize how close we were or how crumbly the ground was at the edge. I remember I had hold of Carolyn and was hurting her and she was trying to get away.

"It's an old trick with children, you know, letting go of the rope all of a sudden and—well, I let go of Carolyn that way. She stumbled backward and tripped and she was so close—she couldn't help herself. She went over the edge."

I was watching her closely and I saw the tremor start as she lost control, but by the time I could reach her, she had gone down on her knees. She went down heavily, blindly, and put out a hand to catch herself. I put my arm around her shoulders but she strained away from me on her knees and the one hand.

"It was as if—" she said, "it was the same as if I had pushed her. It just happened to be the reverse, but it was the same really."

She was shivering. I slid my arm down, got the other one under her knees and picked her up. She was a dead weight. I got her to the couch and covered her to the waist. She lay on her back with her eyes open and her interlaced fingers twisting and curling continuously over her face. Her lips were parted and there was an odor of illness on her breath. I touched her forehead and it was hot. I could feel loose strands of her blond hair. They were stiff, dry feeling, almost like dead hair. She brushed my hand away with unnecessary force. I didn't touch her again.

"You've carried that around all these years," I said.

"Yes. I think it might have been different if someone had come along then, had seen it happen; you know, they might have missed us at the house and come looking—but nobody came. I had to go back all that way, alone. I had to—*tell them!*"

I let the silence run its course. There was time now.

"It was awfully bad then, after I told them. Nobody was angry, nobody scolded me. They just sort of left me alone. I know it wasn't on purpose; there just wasn't time for me then. They fed me and put me to bed and nobody scolded or gave me any mournful talk. I just had it all to myself. I was sick in the night and made a mess on the bed and the floor and nobody scolded me for that either. They just cleaned it up and put me to bed again and took care of me. And every day after that it got a little less bad, little by little, and I learned to live with it as children do. But my mother didn't learn. She died six months later."

"Didn't your mother talk to you about Carolyn's death before she died? Didn't she try to take some of the guilt off your head?"

"Yes, she tried. She told me I mustn't think I had killed Carolyn, that it had been an accident and I ought to think of it that way, because I would have to live a long time with myself. But it didn't convince me. You see, I remembered it so clearly. It couldn't have been an accident. I killed her."

"Still, she might have been right. I knew of a man who remembered distinctly that he had killed his brother by pushing him out of an upstairs window. The truth was that he had been in another part of the house at the time and had looked out just in time to see his brother falling and hear him scream. He had quarreled with his brother that morning. For half his life he carried the guilt for his brother's murder."

She moved her head from side to side in stubborn negation.

"No," she said. "I killed Carolyn."

I let it go. I thought about the man I had mentioned and how unnecessary it had been for him to have that feeling about his brother all that time. Several people could have straightened him out simply by telling him the truth. But he carried it inside himself, so nobody knew he was suffering and so nobody ever told him. He never asked.

"Then I got sick," Dorothy was saying. "Really sick. I was in the hospital for almost a year. I had the best of care but I was alone as never before. There's no loneliness like being sick that way."

"And that was when you began to resurrect Carolyn?" I said.

"Yes. At first it was just the loneliness. When I would pretend very hard that Carolyn was still alive and loved me, I could forget I had killed her. But in order to pretend that hard I had to play at actually being Carolyn. In the hospital, I would be Dorothy being sick and Carolyn would be visiting me. Then I would put on a different color bed jacket and pretend Carolyn was sick and I, Dorothy, was visiting her. Then I did more and more things to be Carolyn, like wearing different clothes and changing my hairdo and I would take turns being Dorothy and Carolyn.

"That's how it started, and after that I never tried to stop it. When we moved here to Chicago, my father put me in a private school and I began making Carolyn into a completely separate person with a whole life of her own. I told my classmates I had a sister who was sort of sick and couldn't go to school but had to stay home and have a tutor. I would even take them home to meet Carolyn. I had made up a story that Carolyn hated me and I could never let her see me around the house because she would fly into a rage and get sick. So I would take them to the house and make them wait while I found out if Carolyn was ready; and then I would play Carolyn for them. Sometimes it was pretty frightening to them. Carolyn wasn't a very nice person."

I noticed she was crying. I could see the sheen of it in her face in the dim light.

"You see, it wasn't enough just to bring Carolyn back to life. I had to make her a different sort of person inside too, and if I made her into a bad girl, it wasn't so bad that I had killed her. I made her into something like a cross I had to bear—my naughty, wayward sister who did bad things and got in trouble, while patient, good Dorothy cleaned up after her."

She fell silent again and it went on for a while.

"When you were playing Carolyn," I said, "did you ever get mixed up? Didn't Dorothy ever try to take over?"

"Sometimes. The first time I ran away from home it was scary. I felt like Carolyn and looked like Carolyn, but every once in a while something would get in the way and I'd be Dorothy, telling Carolyn she was being bad and ought to be ashamed and what if people got suspicious?"

"But nobody did?"

"It was surprisingly easy. I simply became Carolyn, totally. When I introduced myself I believed it and nobody questioned it."

"But then sometimes Dorothy would interfere?"

"Yes. Not so much at first; not when Carolyn was having a lot of fun and excitement. But later, sometimes with Brophy, Dorothy would push in and make Carolyn feel dirty and used up and sick—so sick—"

She was living the whole thing fully now and I could see the retching movements in her throat and diaphragm. She put her hand out gropingly and I gave her mine and she held it beside her on the couch.

"But that never lasted long. Making Carolyn feel that way was the same as killing her all over again."

Her hand was dry and feverish.

"You did awfully well with the masquerade," I said. "How did you manage the quick hair changes—Dorothy blond and Carolyn brunette?"

"They were wigs, Mac. I told you I was sick. I recovered pretty well, but not entirely. I don't—have any hair of my own, Mac. I'm—bald!"

It made my scalp crawl, the way she said it. It must have been harder to tell me that than the rest of it.

"Brophy knew about Carolyn?" I said.

"He found out. I don't know how. I thought at first your friend Henley had told him. I don't think so now. Maybe he made his own investigation."

"Your father must have known—about the double life, I mean. And Brenda?"

"Yes, of course."

"Yet when your father hired Barry Henley to find you, he didn't tell him. He made up something about your being away—"

"Father was just trying to protect me. He thought Mr. Henley would find out where I was and assume I was Carolyn and that would be the end of it."

"Where were you, by the way?"

"In Las Vegas. Getting married." Her tone changed; her eyes came alive. "It was wonderful in Las Vegas!"

She remembered it happily for a minute, then the dullness returned to her eyes.

"And Hayes," I said, "did he know?"

"Foster? I think he suspected, but wasn't sure. I kept my two worlds pretty well clear of each other. Except for a couple of private detectives, and Brophy, I don't think anyone knew."

She squeezed my hand.

"I made quite a mess, didn't I?" she said. "I mean, worse than that. I don't know how to say—"

"Don't say it. Maybe we can get it cleaned up."

She looked at me with mingled hope and fear.

"Is there anything to drink in here?" I asked.

"Yes."

She showed me where to find it. I poured some for both of us. She held the glass carelessly and didn't drink any of it. I did some drinking and quite a lot of thinking about things.

"Do you want out?" I said. "Does Dorothy want out from Brophy?"

"Oh, yes!" she said. "Yes, yes, yes."

"Do you think you can say goodbye to Carolyn now, for good?"

"Yes. I'm sure. I promise."

I thought about it some more.

"You married Brophy under the name of Carolyn Stanhope?"

"Yes."

She watched me hungrily, on one elbow on the couch, holding the glass. Some of it spilled and I took it out of her hand and put it in a safe place.

"Can you do it? Mac, can you help me?"

"Maybe. It will cost some money."

"I don't care—"

"To do it quietly without a nasty fight, I mean. Would it be worth as much as, say, a hundred thousand dollars?"

"More—any amount—"

"I'll need your IOU."

She got up, moved unsteadily to a desk at one side of the room, found a pen and paper. I put the hastily scrawled IOU note in my pocket and helped her back to the couch. She was trembling everywhere. I covered her to the chin. She pushed the blanket down and reached for me with both hands. I leaned close over her.

"Mac—" she said, "will it work? It's like paying blackmail—"

"No. It's a settlement. He won't get anything until after you get your divorce, or annulment. Then he won't be able to come back for more."

"Why not? Why can't he—?"

"Because—listen carefully now—this is the most important thing I will ever tell you, so please get it clear in your mind. You're going to be a big girl from now on, no matter what Brophy does or what anybody else does or says. Whatever dirty past Brophy may shake in your face, you're not going to submit to blackmail. You'll let yourself be exposed if necessary, and it won't be as bad as you think."

"But, Mac—"

"You've been sick. But now you're better, and some day you'll be well altogether. Carolyn was your sickness. We got rid of her tonight—or, say, we got a good start on it. There's no stigma here, no shame. Not for Dorothy."

"I know, but—you don't know Brophy—"

"I have two short words for Brophy. Come on now, cover up and keep warm and let me go. I'll be back."

"Hurry—oh, God, please hurry!"

She clung for a moment. I kissed her face and pulled the blanket up again, covering her. She closed her eyes and lay still. She had a waxy look, doll-like, with that daffodil-colored hair. I wanted to stay with her, but it was time to go.

CHAPTER EIGHTEEN

It was two o'clock in the morning—later. Eddies of raw cold swirled on a stiff east wind. I turned my coat collar up, buried my hands in my pockets and leaned against the old brick wall, looking up to where the light glowed yellowly in Brophy's office.

From half a dozen points, near and distant, came the night sounds: rattle and ring of trash cans, muffled shouts, banging of service doors. A drunk lurched past me, collided with a lamppost and careened backward till he came up against the plate-glass window of a shut-down delicatessen. He stood propped for a moment, then slid slowly to the sidewalk and sprawled on his back. I was glad the window hadn't broken, as I would then have felt it necessary to render assistance. I had problems of my own. I was afraid.

What do I owe Dorothy Stanhope? I thought. I never accepted money from her, nor anything else; not love nor amusement nor any promise of a piece of the future. Miss Jekyll and Mrs. Hyde. If it hadn't been for her crazy neurotic nonsense maybe Barry Henley and Virgie would be alive today—But she didn't know all that, wasn't responsible for it. When Barry found out about her secret life, all she knew was that he was interfering with her, might embarrass her. How could she know about the other?

Still, she had put herself on that hook and maybe she ought to get herself off.

The trouble with that was Brophy. She couldn't get off the hook that was Brophy all by herself.

I don't want to go up there, I thought. Please don't make me go up there. They'll kill me. I'm too old for that one with the big shoulders. They'll wrap me up tight. They'll jam my hat down on my head. They'll dangle me by my heels out the window and when they're ready, they'll let go. There's a chance they won't go that far, but you have to figure they will. I'm a thorn in their rotten flesh and they'll treat me like any thorn, but rougher. Don't make me go up there, please.

There was another voice, too.

Who's making you go up there? Go on home. Call Donovan and let him go up. They won't hurt Donovan.

But Donovan can't handle it. He doesn't know the background.

My hands were wet in my pockets. I took them out and let the icy wind dry them.

You're losing your mind, one of these voices was saying. Pull it together, man. Figure it out. Go up there or go home, but don't stand on the dirty street and take pneumonia.

Heroism is for heroes, I thought.

All right then, go home.

I can't. There's nobody waiting for me at home.

I give up on you, it said.

She could go back to Las Vegas and get a divorce all on her own. She can afford it.

But if Brophy fights it—

You can't clean up everybody's mess. She made it herself.

Brophy helped.

Then go deal with Brophy.

Nobody can deal with Brophy. Brophy makes the whole world helpless. Brophy and those guys have got the world by the little hairs.

No they haven't. Say it's a standoff. Even odds. There aren't any better.

Brophy names his own odds.

One of the voices said the two words about Brophy. One of them was his name. It was spoken aloud and I looked both ways along the street to see who might have heard. I looked down at the passed-out lush and he hadn't heard.

It would be nice if he turned out to be Brophy, I thought. I could drop a rock on him and get on home.

I don't know about it is the trouble, the legal part of it. Maybe Brophy knows more law than I do. I need a lawyer.

Why not?

Pretty funny.

On the other hand, maybe you have just talked yourself into a total solution.

I took a small walk, thinking it over. It got pretty exciting. I kicked it along the gutter like it was a tin can. I mauled it over like a cat worrying a spool of thread. I unwound it and wound it up again and it was as tight as ever. It was beautiful. It would take a little talking, but talk is cheap. Somebody said that. Somebody is always saying that, largely because it's true. Compared with anything else you can name, talk is cheaper.

I had to walk eight blocks to find anyone to talk to. It turned out to be a bartender in an otherwise deserted joint. He was reading a newspaper and when I ordered a slug of bourbon, he sighed heavily and looked at his watch.

"It won't take long," I said.

He blinked at me.

"Telephone?" I asked.

He nodded toward a dark corner and I saw a phone on the wall. I talked him out of some change, threw down the slug and went over there. I dialed Budge's office. It rang about ten times and somebody picked it up.

"Hi—Safford?" I said.

"Oh, yes," he said. "How are you, Mac?"

"Just fine. Is Budge there?"

"No."

"Is he reachable?"

"Well, I guess so—it depends."

"This is kind of hot, so maybe I should give it to you and you could call Budge."

"Sure, go ahead."

"Like this," I said, wide awake now with only one voice in my head, laying it down carefully along the thin, taut line. "You know about Brophy. Some way, I don't know how, he stumbled onto this later Stanhope will, the one we were talking about the other day. The earlier will, of course, is much more advantageous to Brophy, if he can make his marriage stick. Oh I forgot to mention, Brophy is married to the Stanhope girl. Dorothy—or Carolyn— they're both the same girl."

"No kidding," he said.

"Yeah. So she wants out and I'm supposed to make a deal with Brophy. Now I don't have a copy of that later will, the one Barry Henley witnessed just before Stanhope died, but I think I can lay my hands on it. But for to-night, we don't need it. What I'm getting at, I'm about to go up and negoti-ate with Brophy to get Dorothy Stanhope out of that marriage. I can talk to Brophy all right in his own language, but I'm not too strong on the legal aspects. I'd like Budge to come along with me. You too, if you can make it."

"At this hour of the night?" he said. "What—?"

"These guys live all night," I said. "You have to catch them where they are. Besides, the Stanhope estate will be coming out of court any minute, starting tomorrow, and it has to be wrapped up. So if you'll call Budge—"

"I don't know, Mac. At this hour and all—"

"There'll be a handsome fee in it," I said. "The Stanhope woman is prepared to pay."

"Well—"

"So give Budge a ring, huh, and meet me in front of the B and D Hotel and Restaurant Supply Company as soon as you can make it. I'll be wait-ing on the street. I don't want to get up there and start saying all the wrong things."

"Well—I'll call him and see—"

"Good. So long for now."

I hung up. I went back to the bar and I felt pretty good. One more slug to tighten me up against the cold and I could ride out the night. It would be either very short or very long and it didn't matter too much, just so they wouldn't hang me out that window by the ankles.

I lingered over the shot and the bartender kept looking at his watch and pretty soon he got to wandering around making big, banging, closing noises. But it was warm in there and I had a tendency to dawdle.

I thought about Dorothy Stanhope off and on. If it should work out that she would have to go to Las Vegas to get an annulment, maybe she would need a bodyguard. I made a good bodyguard, especially on the candlelight and champagne circuit. And the weather is nice out there, none of this standing around with your hands in your pockets.

I started the cold walk back to Brophy's place. It would take Budge and Safford about half an hour to forty-five minutes, depending on whether Budge was asleep when Safford called him. About all I had left to worry about was whether Brophy would hang around his office long enough. I went around to the alley and looked up and the light still glowed on the ninth floor. I crossed back to the vicinity of the delicatessen across the street. The drunk had moved over into the doorway and was asleep sitting up against the wall. I carried on a brief struggle with my conscience and won it. The hell with him. He stank.

I tried to put myself in Barry Henley's shoes, wondering whether he had stood in this same spot with the same expectations, the same fears. Brophy probably wasn't any tougher now than he had been then. Maybe Barry had died because he had gone at it the wrong way. Maybe he had climbed the fire ladder to that little balcony and had thrown rocks at Brophy's window and tried to talk to him across the alley canyon.

But there was Virgie and she hadn't made any mistakes—unless it had been a mistake to come to me. That could have been a big one.

So the big wheel turned and finally came around and I had the spur where I needed it. The hell with Dorothy Stanhope; she would always get along. But there had been Virgie and before her, Barry, and I owed it to both of them.

It was primitive, but it worked. All of a sudden,, standing there with the smell of the city in my nose-and the wind whistling down my neck, I was prepared. I had a feeling of elation. It was my city and I was in charge. I had the drop on the entire congregation. One word from me, one gesture, everything under control. A few forceful, quiet phrases, and—

Then the waiting part was over. I watched the quiet, rabbit-like approach of the big Cadillac, dwarfed by the trucks and warehouses that lined its route. I tossed a glance upward. Brophy's light still showed. I started over to meet them and they climbed out of the car, Budge on the off side and Safford from under the wheel.

We stood in a spare huddle, looking across at the B and D Hotel and Restaurant Supply Company. Budge was fidgety.

"I'm afraid I don't follow this too well," he said. "Eric called me and—"

"I asked him to," I said. "Did he explain?"

"Well—"

"About the will and all."

"Yes, but—"

"The thing is," Safford said, "we don't understand what we have to do with Brophy. It looks as if you may be using us to pull your own chestnuts out of the fire."

"Maybe," I said, "but there's bound to be something in it." Rushing it to keep them from getting too preoccupied with the late hour and the fuzziness of the situation, I said, "I did hold out one thing on you."

"What?" Budge asked sharply.

His gray face looked old and defeated in the emaciated light of the street.

"I do have a copy of that second will."

They just looked at me.

"I held out," I said, "because I was afraid if I told you I had it, you wouldn't come. We'll use it as a lever to pry Brophy loose from Dorothy Stanhope. I'm sure it will work, but I need legal advice."

"I'm afraid," Budge said stiffly, "that I don't know enough about the relationships here to be much help. As for the will—"

"After," I said. "After we've dealt with Brophy, we'll get the later will into court. Miss Stanhope is resigned to accepting the inheritance in the form of a trust fund. But there's this Brophy thing and she's willing to pay a good solid price for that; at least a hundred thousand."

I brought out the IOU she had written me and made them look at it.

"That's as good as cash, men," I said.

"But, Mac—" Budge said.

"Where's the copy of the will?" Safford asked.

"In my car," I said. "It's kind of hot. I had to steal it out of Miss Lundquist's desk and it's the only one in existence that I know of, so I didn't want to carry it around."

"Miss Stanhope knows about the will then?" Budge said.

"Yeah. Just among us," I said, "I was tempted to perform a little extortion on Miss Stanhope. I thought it might be worth a lot to her to have this later will just ignored and forgotten. In fact, I was dreaming around in the neighborhood of a million bucks. But then I chickened out. I'm a small-time operator. Big money makes me nervous. So if we can collect, say, a hundred grand among the three of us, it would be a nice fee and no involvement. Everything honest and clean and no bad dreams. Okay? Let's walk down and get the copy. Then we're in."

"But—" Budge said.

"Sure," Safford cut in. "Let's go."

I started out briskly and they came along, just keeping up.

"A man can work a long time before he gets a break like this one," I said, talking to Budge. "You know how it goes. You sweat it out twenty, thirty years for peanuts and then all of a sudden you hit a good one and you're all set."

I don't know why I'm so chatty all of a sudden, I thought, and then I thought, Yes, you do, you know exactly why. Hang onto it.

We were a dozen paces short of my parked car when the prowl wagon drifted around the corner behind us, rolled past us slowly, started past my car, then stopped, rocking forward gently and settling back. Safford swore under his breath.

"It's all right," I said.

"After all," Budge said, "it's not illegal to walk the public street, I hope."

A uniformed officer got out on the off side of the prowl car and strolled diagonally to the curb. I met him at my right front fender.

"Your car?" he said.

"Yes, officer," I said.

"It's in a loading zone."

"Sorry, I didn't notice. It was midnight, no traffic; just careless of me."

"Uh-huh," he said. He looked past me at Safford and Budge and at the car for a minute and then at me again. "Better move it," he said.

"Right away."

He looked us over again and I waited respectfully while he walked back to the car, where the radio sputtered unintelligibly. There was one in plain clothes in the back seat, but everything was in the way and all I could see of him was the brim of his hat.

Budge had his collar up to his ears and was shivering with his hands in his pockets. Safford was standing around.

"I'll get the document," I said.

The prowl car drifted to the next corner and turned right. I opened the car from the curb side and Safford said, "Aren't you going to move the car?"

"Unh-uh," I said. "This whole block is either red zone or loading. I could drive around for ten minutes looking for a legal slot. The hell with it."

I leaned in and fiddled with my keys and got the glove compartment open. Reaching in, I thought how convenient it was to have a stock of slightly worn envelopes on hand. You never know but what you might want to mail something.

I got one in my hand, banged the compartment shut and started to back out of the car in that awkward way you have to, stooped and off balance. After a moment I came up against a thin, prodding obstruction. When I pushed a little, it pricked like a rose thorn in the soft of my back under the ribs. I stood still.

"Come on out," Safford said, "slowly."

"Wait a minute—!" I said indignantly.

"Come on!"

I went back some more and the knife yielded inch by inch.

"Listen—" Budge whispered fiercely.

"Shut up," Safford said. "This is it, the last chance. Remember?" He nudged me.

I hadn't expected a knife. The rest of it, but not the knife. I had the envelope in my hand and when I started to turn, Safford snatched it and turned with me, staying behind.

"Over against the wall," he said.

The sharp nudge of the knife was the authority. I walked over there and put my hands flat against the brick, waiting. Sweat prickled on my face and elsewhere. I had lost some confidence. Maybe the rest would go wrong too.

"Budge," I said, "you're in deep. Talk to your boy. There's no million in it any more. I wasn't feeding you any line about that. The girl won't go for it."

"Shut up," Safford said. "Here, hold this—"

His breath was on the back of my neck. I could feel the knife at the fleshy pad under my rib.

"Talk to him, Budge," I said. "Who's the boss at your place?"

But we knew that, didn't we? How a man can let himself be taken over by the slow, certain attrition of mediocrity, the frustration of an inadequate career.

My hands against the brick were cold stumps.

But I doubt, I thought, that Safford would drop me right here after that heaven-sent night prowler had such a good long look at all of us.

But he might.

"We're going to get in your car," Safford growled, "and drive around. You'll turn and walk over there slowly and not do anything foolish."

"You can't make it," I said.

"I think so. I think you're the only one left who knows enough to make a case. And they don't execute attorneys for killing private eyes in self-defense."

"With a knife?" I said. "Come on, Safford. Everybody knows. Donovan knows."

"No, he doesn't. He would have picked us up by now."

"I told him to hold off a while."

It was the weakest argument I could have made.

"All right, turn around, to your left, slowly, out from the wall."

He pricked me with the needlelike point. I turned. He was alert as a cat. With all his size and the close quarters, since he grabbed the envelope I hadn't seen any part of him. He had become the knife, as every killer, every suicide, becomes the instrument of destruction—a rope, a gun, a bottle of nitro, a stick of dynamite. Or a bottle of whisky, a nine-million horsepower automobile…

We were moving toward the car. Once in there it would all be in Safford's hands.

So on your feet, philosopher. It's a way of dying. Live like a dumb private eye with your hands in the soft of his throat and your knee in his groin, but do it fast. Do it like a Brophy.

Then it happened. I had planned on it, then hoped for it, and finally I had given up, and it happened. Budge chickened out.

"Now, hold on," he said, "this is foolish. Put that thing away and let's work it out—"

But Safford was wholly committed. His voice had a lashing hoarseness.

"You get in there and start that car," he said to Budge. "Right now!"

The needle jabbed me and I moved from it.

"No!" Budge said. "And after him, then me, is that it? Give me that knife."

I heard the scrape of his foot and felt the lunge as Safford held him off. I stepped forward to get clear, spun around and Budge was grabbing awkwardly for the big man's wrist. Safford hit him with his free hand and Budge sprawled on the cement. I ducked under Safford's arm and reached up, got hold of it. When I tried to twist it, he jerked free and squared off at me, the long arm out for the lunge. He was as big as a house. Budge was getting up warily.

"All right," Safford said, beckoning. "You want it like that? Come on—" I started in, stopped short and made a pass to his midsection. He twisted, off balance, and I got hold of his knife hand and wrist and hung on. I raised it and brought it down and then up in back and he hollered, but wouldn't drop the knife. I yanked him back onto my knee and it dropped. He whirled desperately and stumbled back against the wall, nursing his dislocated arm. I felt something on my shoulder and ducked. Budge spoke quietly.

"Mac, wait—let's make a deal—"

"Shut up," I said.

I moved on Safford and he kicked at me. His head swiveled one way, then the other. He broke and ran; not in a straight line; toward the corner where we had left the car. A uniformed cop came around it on his toes and ready to go. Safford halted, spun and started down the other way. A big man in a plain business suit and another uniformed officer came around the far corner.

It was Donovan who collared Safford, pushing with both big hands, racking him up against the wall. We were stretched out along the block like outnumbered pickets in dispersal. There was a brief tableau. Then the three of us and the three of them gathered and tightened and moved together along the wall till we met in a neutral zone on the black facade of the warehouse.

"Him, too," I said, pointing to Budge.

The officer looked to Donovan, who nodded. He took handcuffs from his belt and hooked the lawyer's wrists together. Budge leaned against the wall, looking down at his hands.

"I'm glad it's over," he said.

They didn't bother with manacles for Safford. His arm was useless. You could hear his pain between his teeth.

Donovan and I wandered down to the curb, where I did some routine spitting. Donovan was ominously silent. I braced myself.

"There's a character," he said finally, "hangs around botherin' at me—a detective story writer."

I waited.

"I thought up a good one for him," Donovan said. "Death of a Lone Wolf.'"

"Corny," I said, "but true."

"What if I wouldn't have been staked out on Budge? What if I was sittin' around havin' a few beers?"

"I might have got killed."

"You got a license to operate a one-man vigilante society?"

"No, sir."

"That big one—you got him so desperate he might have killed a policeman tryin' to get away."

"I realize that."

"It was a dumb, stupid, bull-headed way to do, wasn't it?"

"Yes, sir."

"Is that what you got a license for?"

"No, sir."

"All right, you remember it."

"Try and make me forget it."

We started back to where one of the officers was standing with Safford and Budge, waiting for the other one to bring up the car.

"By the way," I said, "how come you were staked out on Budge?"

"I see them drive away from your place Sunday."

"Well, but—"

"Tonight I get a call from some girl—you remember that little nurse with the freckles that was in the hospital—"

"I remember."

"She was real upset. She said she couldn't get hold of you anywhere and she had to tell somebody that the big guy who was fixing the Cadillac in front of your place was the same one she saw riggin' the Henley woman's car."

Budge was looking at me.

"When did you know?" he asked.

There was no way to be with him but gentle. They had him. He was finished.

"Barry Henley had to have come into possession of something valuable," I said. "It turned out to be that will. Barry would naturally have consulted you about it. When it didn't show up in his files, and after Brophy's people went to all that trouble to find it and couldn't, I could only figure Barry had turned it over to you for safekeeping.

"It must have hit you right away that it might be worth a fortune to Dorothy Stanhope. But even with Barry out of the way, you couldn't use it till the other copies had been accounted for and you didn't know where they were. For all you knew, they might turn up at any moment, go through the regular channels and supersede the earlier will in a normal way. Then there would no longer be any chance to sell your one copy to Dorothy. You had to hang onto it and sweat it out till the last minute, keeping your eye on the condition of the Stanhope estate. If it should appear at the last minute that nobody was going to come forward with the later will, then you could move in. I imagine you lost your own taste for it in a hurry and would have given it up, but then Safford came into it. Safford had drive and ambition. But it was a big chunk of money and even he could bide his time.

"Then when you heard from Virgie that somebody was snooping around her apartment, you could figure it was the will they were after. She might know about it. Just her knowing about it was a threat. She could put the big hitch in your plans whether she had a copy of the will or not. All she would have to do would be to tell somebody about it; somebody like me. Virgie had told you she was coming to see me. She hadn't told anybody else, except her apartment manager. And it was in front of my office she was killed."

I moved over and looked at Safford against the wall. His arm was giving him hell and I couldn't have cared less.

"Why?" I said. "Why Virgie? She had been in contact with me for more than twenty-four hours before you did it. If she was going to tell me about the will, she would have done it long since. It was that you didn't know about it right away, wasn't it? Budge wasn't going to tell you about Virgie and me. You wormed it out of him."

He didn't say anything. It was just as well.

"It began to look like Safford was in it," I said, "when I was in your office the second time. I asked him casually about looking into an estate matter and he knew which one I meant even before I mentioned the name, though he had claimed to know nothing about the Stanhope case at all. That was the day he told me he had learned several trades, working his way through school. This clicked when I watched him fix your carburetor that Sunday afternoon.

"You," I said to Budge, "you must have wanted to get caught. When you came to tell me about your visit to Miss Lundquist, I asked you if Miss Stanhope was home and you said yes, that you met her. This couldn't have been possible because at that moment, I was buying a bottle of champagne for Miss Stanhope at the 401 Club. Of course, I didn't know what I was doing until later; tonight."

I was tired of it. The officer had brought up the car. I stepped back. Budge's eyes followed me hungrily.

"Did you push Barry Henley off that building?" I asked him.

"No," he said. "I swear it, Mac! He fell. He took me up there to show me something across the way, in Brophy's place. He fell. I don't know how. There wasn't anything I could do."

"And he had already given you the will, asked your advice about it?"

"Yes."

"And he told you Carolyn Stanhope was married to Brophy?"

"Yes."

"But not that there was really only one Stanhope girl."

"No, not that."

"So as time went by and the other copies of that will didn't turn up, you arranged to tip off Brophy to their existence, figuring he would try to find them."

"Eric did it. I—"

"Shut up!" Safford said, gritting his teeth.

I looked at Budge for a minute.

"I'm sorry about everything," I said.

I walked away to the curb again, not wanting to watch them put into the car. Donovan joined me and did a little spitting of his own.

"You all wrapped up on this now?" he said.

"Sure. Why not?"

"You had a beef cooking with Brophy."

"Oh—that."

"No need to bother with that now, huh?"

I had never outright lied to him. I had evaded and begged off and held my peace, but I had never actually lied.

"It won't take long," I said, "while I'm in the neighborhood."

He sighed raucously.

"You gonna try for it twice in one night?"

"I hate these loose ends. Starting tomorrow I have to get to work for money."

"Look, they'll slap your ears off. They will lay you out on the long ice."

"I plan to reform them."

"You do, huh? With what kind of equipment?"

"The best kind," I said. "Money."

He straightened from the wall in a funny kind of indignant shrug.

"Hell," he said, "I can't stand around here arguin' with a bull-headed private eye. I got things to do."

"Well, good night, Lieutenant."

"Good night, Genius. I'll send your clothes to the Goodwill."

He moved fast to the car and got in and slammed the door. He didn't do any looking back.

I waited till they had disappeared around the corner. Then I crossed the street to the B and D Hotel and Restaurant Supply Company. There was a bell beside the plate-glass door, but I doubted they would come all the way down from the ninth floor to answer it. There was a telephone number for emergencies on the piece of cardboard stuck under the bell, but I decided it would take too long to arouse Brophy's interest by that roundabout route. I prowled around the street till I found a loose brick and I went back and stood off about eight or ten feet and heaved it through the glass. I reached through the hole in the door and tripped the locks and walked in.

CHAPTER NINETEEN

It was dark in there and I stumbled a few times as I picked my way among the thousand and one useful articles that Brophy had for sale. A couple of them were noisy, but nobody showed up to investigate. I wished I had brought something with which to protect myself in case they were waiting for me upstairs. I caught sight of a display of kitchenware and when I went over for a closer look, one of the items was a handsome, stainless steel meat cleaver. I picked it up and got into the elevator with it.

At the ninth floor I got out and walked into the little reception office, feeling foolish because I still had the meat cleaver and nobody was waiting for me. I went over to Brophy's door and used it to knock with. I could only knock once. The cleaver buried itself in the panel and stuck there.

"Who is it?" Brophy said from inside.

"It's me," I said.

Somebody opened the door. Whisky Davis. I walked in past him while he worked his throat to get his voice box started.

"What the hell—" Brophy was at his desk in shirtsleeves, peering through his glasses. There were some ledgers open in front of him. The lad with the shoulders was not in sight. I also missed the girl with the orange hair.

"How'd you get in here?" Brophy said thinly.

"You ought to do something about that front door," I said. "If I'd had a van I could have cleaned you out."

"What do you want?"

"All right if I sit down?" I said.

They didn't say anything, so I sat down. Brophy leaned forward across his desk, took off his glasses and squeezed his eyes together with his fingers.

"I got maybe two minutes for you," he said.

"It will take longer."

"You see if you can't squeeze it in."

I took off my hat and held it between my knees.

"We just killed your wife," I said. "Carolyn. There was no pain. We liquidated her with a few choice phrases and laid her to rest without ritual. She is no longer in existence."

Brophy's face didn't change. I couldn't even be sure he was listening.

"The thing I'm getting around to," I said, "is that, as we know, Carolyn never did exist. That is, she did for a while, but that was a long time ago. But the Carolyn you married was a fictitious person. Therefore, logically, you are not married to a woman named Carolyn Stanhope at all."

Brophy pushed himself backward in slow motion till his swivel chair rocked into the reclining position. He crossed his legs and tapped with his glasses on his knee.

"You got about half a minute more," he said. "I hope you can get to the payoff of your joke by then."

"No joke," I said. "And the time you use to talk back ought not to count. The trouble here is that 'logically' and 'legally' are two different things. You went through a legal ceremony with a woman who claimed to be Carolyn Stanhope, and who bore a striking resemblance to Miss Dorothy Stanhope. How could you know there wasn't any such person as the girl you married?"

He pulled a cloth from his pocket, cleaned his glasses and put them on. He smiled at me blandly.

"Go ahead," he said. "Give me the pitch. I can't wait."

I was scared. It's always preferable to have them react by the book, snotty and tough. Brophy was giving me the happiness technique.

"It would be a lot of trouble and expense," I said, "for Dorothy Stanhope to get clear of this marriage by a public brawl in a local court. We think she would win, but it would be better to do it more quietly, say by an uncontested divorce in Nevada, under the name of Carolyn Stanhope. Inasmuch as Dorothy Stanhope is soon to come into about two million dollars, this might demand a little forbearance on your part."

"It might," Brophy agreed.

"We are therefore prepared to offer a substantial settlement, in cash."

He was still smiling. I felt something crawl up my spine and crawl down again and I shifted uneasily and ran my finger under my collar. Whisky Davis was standing to the southeast of my left knee, cleaning his fingernails with a pocket knife.

"How much?" Brophy said.

"How much do you want?"

"One million dollars," he said. "I'll listen."

I stood up, twirled my hat once around my finger and put it on. I turned to the door.

"We didn't have such a figure in mind," I said. "I guess we'll have to fight it out."

"It would be a dirty fight," he said.

"I know. But I ought to tell you that Dorothy Stanhope is a big girl now. She'll take a chance on the publicity. If she has to do a Lady Godiva down Michigan Avenue, she'll do it. She figures she owes that much to the memory of her sister."

All of a sudden I was yelling in a dream. I was the only one who could hear me. Whisky Davis went on cleaning his nails. Brophy sat back in his swivel chair giving me that bland look. I had threatened to cut him off right where it would hurt the most, right across the pockets, and he was impervious to my threat. And an impervious gangster is one who has to be disarmed like a bomb, tenderly and with care, infinite care.

I had been confident he wouldn't go so far as to rub me out on the spot. Now I wasn't so sure. His face opened. He spoke in an even, quiet, almost friendly way.

"You're pretty good," he said, "in your line. You got a stubborn streak. You remind me of one of these Boston bulldogs, you know, the little ones with the teeth. You go in there with your little chin sticking out and you keep goin' back and you stay in there all the way, huh?"

I looked at him carefully. So far, he hadn't been too unpleasant. But I had seen his type self-lashed to homicidal fury, and Brophy might run to type.

"Everybody makes a living," I said.

He grinned.

"Yeah," he said. "How much living do you make, bulldog? In a week, a month? You talk about two million dollars like you knew what it was. How much? How much would you cost me, say, if I had any use for you? Forty a week, say? Forty dollars a week! How's that? You can start tomorrow."

"It would have to be negotiated," I said.

He kept grinning.

"I might have a job for you at that," he said. "I can always use collectors. They tell me you're an honest man. I wouldn't have to worry. If you worked out on collections you could move up in the organization. You could be a salesman, on commissions. How about that?"

"Let me think it over," I said.

He nodded, grinning.

"Sure, think it over, bulldog. Let me hear from you."

In the midst of a silence that was nearly a perfect vacuum, I heard the elevator rumble to life. Someone downstairs had sent for it. If it was my friend Mr. America, he would have entered the building by the door I had broken, and when he reached the outer office, he would see the meat cleaver sticking in the door. It was easy to rationalize that I couldn't accomplish anything more here.

"All right," I said, reaching for the doorknob. "You think it over about the Stanhope proposition. If you want me, I'm in the book."

Brophy chuckled.

"Sure," he said, "but don't run off. Hang around a few minutes. Have a drink."

Whisky Davis put his penknife in his pocket and cleared his throat.

"Thanks just the same," I said, "but it's getting late—"

Whisky Davis had moved silently to lean against the door. He didn't interfere with me in any other way, but it was clear that if I should start to open the door, I would be at quite a disadvantage, position-wise.

I slid to one side and turned my back to the wall beside it. Brophy had come up with a bottle of Scotch, planting it in the middle of his big desk.

"Whisky," he said, "get some glasses."

"Sure," Whisky croaked. It was the fourth word he had spoken since my arrival, the first three having been "What the hell."

The sound of the elevator had faded, but now it resumed and was coming back, rising in pitch to a high humming sound. I stood by the door, waiting for it to stop, and for the sound of the doors sliding and the footsteps; waiting for Mr. America, who was one round down in our tournament and might feel impelled to even the score.

Whisky Davis set out some glasses in a crystal semicircle around the long-necked bottle. They were nice glasses with heavy bottoms and light fluting. They could probably be had for about eight-fifty a dozen, whether you wanted them or not.

"You like Scotch," Brophy told me.

"Sure," I said, "why not?"

"Come and get it," he said.

He poured generously. The elevator had stopped. I didn't hear the doors because I was walking over to the big desk and picking up my drink.

"Down the hatch," Brophy said, raising his glass.

"Yeah," I said.

Somebody tapped on the door.

"What?" Brophy called.

The voice of Mr. America came through the panel, tight and cautious.

"Okay in there?" he said.

"Everything is okay," Brophy said. "Come on in."

I stood there with the heavy shot glass in my hand, watching the knob turn and the door open and Mr. America looking in carefully under the still imbedded cleaver. He saw we were in order, stepped back and disappeared.

Dorothy Stanhope came in. Or Carolyn. Or both. The brunette came in. She slipped in shyly, her gaze falling from mine as our eyes met and she looked at Brophy and nodded to Whisky and moved a little to one side to let in Mr. America with her overnight bag.

She was wearing a mink coat and black gloves and carrying a black patent leather purse with both hands in front of her. She looked like a girl coming in too late from the prom.

"Hi, honey," Brophy said behind me. "Have a drink."

She shifted her purse, walked to the desk and picked up a glass. Her eyes lifted with it and met mine again.

"I'm sorry, Mac," she said. "I guess this is where I really belong."

I choked down the rest of my slug and headed for the door. Whisky Davis and Mr. America watched me. The latter even took a couple of steps, but Brophy mumbled something and he stopped. I opened the door, then hesitated and looked back, because the hope never really dies till you take that long last breath. I looked at Dorothy-Carolyn Stanhope exclusively and I guess my eyes said something, because hers twitched a little, then slid away. Then she looked at me once more and shook her head slightly.

"I'm sorry," she said. "Thanks for trying."

I shrugged and opened the door all the way.

"I guess you can't win 'em all," I said.

I went out and through the reception office and got in the elevator. There was a light on the main floor and it wasn't any trick to cross it and make the door and get outside in the fresh, fresh air.

"Anybody can get dynamite," Donovan had said.

Anybody can get knives, machine guns, bazookas, flame throwers; pretty soon now anybody can get atomic warheads, nuclear pellets—

Think not?

Who will be watching?

I stood there in front of Brophy's store, watching a car coming down the empty street from the west. It was coming fast and swerving a lot. I thought how lucky it was for the driver that it happened to be a quiet hour. Under the circumstances, he had a bare chance of living a couple of minutes longer.

He was even with me when he put on the brakes. It was a big, heavy, expensive car and it rocked and slid on the pavement, the tires groaning, tortured. It headed into the curb, rode up over it with one wheel and stalled when the other hit the obstruction. It was still rocking a little when the door opened and a guy got out and stumbled around the back end of it, supporting himself drunkenly with one hand, moving toward where I stood. He paused, catching sight of me, and I saw his face in a dingy light. It was Foster Hayes.

I started down to meet him and he came on, making it all right to the nearest lamppost, where he grabbed and hung on. I could see him fine then. He had been brutally dealt with. His face resembled a pink-tinted egg yolk, half boiled. He peered at me through a slit between puffed eyelids. There was a deep cut on the side of his face and blood on his neck that had run down from the ear that appeared half severed. His mouth was swollen twice normal, and when he spoke he chewed his words out through broken teeth. I put a hand out to help him and he shrugged away from it.

"Is she in there?" he mumbled.

"Look," I said, "you need a doctor. Let me help you into the car—"

He brushed me off savagely and straightened away from the post.

"Who did it?" I said.

"Fellow came to get Dorothy—big fellow—"

"You tangled with that pro? You crazy?"

"Tried to stop him—no match—took Dorothy. I followed 'em—"

"You know where we are?" I asked.

"Sure—that gangster—Brophy."

He pushed himself away from the post and headed crazily on an erratic slant for the B and D place. I caught up with him.

"Take it easy," I said. "Let's work it out."

He started fighting me.

"I'll kill the dirty sonsabitches—" he croaked.

"All right, we'll do it together," I said.

I backed off, giving way slowly, letting him work off that steam he had left. He couldn't hurt me, but he could hurt himself now, as near blind as he was. I gave him back his gold star with a bonus. He made up for plenty in heart.

My left heel came up against the first step of the store entrance and I swung around to keep my balance. Hayes floundered past me, stumbled on the steps and went down. That seemed to do it. He lay there and scratched at the concrete with his fingernails and I heard him mumbling. I got hold of his arm, gently.

"It's all right," I said. "It's not your business to fight with your hands. Come on inside."

"Dorothy—" he mumbled, "stopped fight—only for me—I would have killed the—"

I leaned down close, so he wouldn't miss it with his bad ear.

"I'll get Dorothy for you," I said. "Now come on inside so I'll know where you are."

He made the last good try and helped himself up through the door into the warehouse. The place looked like a monster dollhouse in the yellowish light somebody had turned on, presumably Mr. America on his earlier entrance. Off to the far right, at a maximum distance from the elevator, was a cluster of divans and settees with svelte plastic upholsteries. I worked Foster Hayes in that direction, half leading, half supporting him. He came along all right, stumbling now and then. He kicked over a couple of spindly floor lamps but the clatter didn't bother me. They were nine floors up and I had said goodbye.

I selected a long davenport and helped him onto it. He lay down all right, then started up, fighting again, and I held him.

"It's all right," I said. "Stay here. Whatever happens, whatever you hear, just stay."

"Dorothy—" he mumbled again.

"I'm going to get her now," I promised.

It would be a pleasure, I thought, walking away. That was some girl, that Dorothy. She must have been ready to gag right in their faces, walking in that way with that wonderful actress face of hers, saying, "I guess this is where I belong." Belong indeed. But she had fooled me. They sent Mr. America to fetch her and Hayes fought for her. He might have won—or he might have been killed, and she couldn't let that happen. So to put a stop to it, she had voluntarily walked back into the Brophy sewer; only to find me in the same spot Hayes had been in a few minutes before. And I would have fought for her too, only she was such a good actress, and she saved my skin too. So she had something coming, if only a little of my skin, and maybe it wasn't too late. I wondered if Brophy would fight for her, too. We would see.

And if I don't do this right, I also thought, I'll lose more skin than I can afford. I'm going to have to draw those two out. I don't want to go wandering into their den, where they're at home. They got to come out.

CHAPTER TWENTY

I stood in the middle of the cluttered room and spotted the passages in and out. In addition to the street entrance, there were two: the elevator, and the wide double door where the stairway came down and the service entrance shared space with it. The service entrance was at a right angle to the elevator, in the far wall opposite the davenport section where I had stashed Hayes.

Along the front wall beside the door were shelves stocked with china and glassware. I went down there and pretty soon I found an aluminum tray such as is used for carrying drinking glasses among other items. I couldn't find any of those ordinary heavy-duty, cafeteria type glasses, but I didn't look very hard. There were plenty of fancy ones—cocktail, champagne and such, with long, slender stems, delicately fluted. I wondered if Brophy was proud of them.

I loaded up the tray and carried it over to the service desk near the door. There was a small telephone switchboard behind the desk. After a short investigation, I found that the trunk line was disconnected, which was fine. All I needed was the interior system. I opened the switch and started yanking and feeding in plugs, watching the lights flash on and off, hearing buzzers, some nearby, some remote. I kept experimenting till all the buzzings stopped, then fed in some more plugs and let them ring. The operator's earphone and mouthpiece was lying on a shelf beside the instrument. I pulled it over to where I could make some use of it. After about a minute, it started to sputter. I picked it up. Over it came the unmistakable, scratchy voice of Whisky Davis.

"What the hell—!" he said, and that fitted.

I told him who it was. He sputtered. I put the thing down, went over to the shelf and got the tray loaded with glassware and carried it back to the switchboard. Balancing it on one hand, I picked up the mouthpiece.

"Listen," I said, "I'm about to take the place apart. You want to come down and help?"

I waited till he stopped sputtering again. Then I slowly tipped the tray until the merchandise slid off, headed for the concrete floor. For good measure I dropped the mouthpiece along with it. It made a lot of noise, even without benefit of amplification. To Davis it would sound like an automobile crash at close range.

I left the junk where I had dumped it, got over to a panel of light switches just inside the desk area and found the one that worked on the main floor.

In the sudden dark, everything in the room turned to gray shadows.

I found my way back to the center of the room. An open aisle, formed by miscellaneous merchandise lined up along each side, led from the front door to the elevator. There were mostly lamps on one side and some bar stools and Oriental folding screens on the other. One row back on each side were a couple of square columns supporting the ceiling. I headed for the nearest, not far on a slant from the elevator, and about thirty feet into the room from the service entrance and stairway. They would have to come from one or the other.

Or maybe they would split up on the second or third floor and come in both ways at once. I ran my tongue over my lips and wondered which would come from which door. It would be nice, I thought, if Davis would come by the elevator. It would be easier all around if I could handle him first. But they might figure that out and do it the other way around. In either case, one of them anyway was bound to be heeled. Maybe both. And they could shoot me and get away with it because I was on their property, having broken and entered.

I tried not to think about that. I heard some sound behind me and jumped like a deer. It was Hayes, mumbling.

"Stay there," I growled at him. "Everything will be all right. Please stay put."

That was a pretty good line, I thought, that "everything will be all right" bit.

Distantly there was the sound of the elevator. I couldn't see the indicator in the dark, so I couldn't tell whether it was going up or coming down. A red exit sign over the service entrance glowed like an evil eye. Both big doors were closed, but I would be able to tell when they opened. Likewise, I would be able to tell when the elevator reached the main floor. So it didn't matter a lot whether it was going up or coming down at the moment; but it would have been nice to know. I wished I had put Hayes into his car, because with him in the store with me, I would have to account for both of them more or less permanently.

I went to the vicinity where I had found the meat cleaver, moving backward, crabwise, feeling my way. I couldn't find anything except more cleavers and I wasn't up to hacking at people. I gave up the idea and got back to my pillar. I had the basic advantage that I wasn't going after them; they were coming after me, in a dark room. They could hurt me all right, but they would have to find me first: repeat, *first*.

Behind me, Hayes choked, possibly on one of his own teeth, and had a coughing spell. I couldn't bring myself to tell him to shut up. I put both hands flat against the pillar and waited it out. When it stopped, I wiped my hands on my pants and went on waiting. My eyes began to water, staring at the place where the elevator indicator should have been, trying to see it. Maybe they would forgo the elevator entirely and the two of them would come down the stairs. That would not be so good. My hands were sweating again and I gave up trying to outguess them and just waited, hanging onto the pillar.

But if there's another light switch out in that service area, I thought, I'm cooked.

The elevator was humming again, a little louder each second. I fixed my eyes on the service door, watching for a change in the pattern of light and shadow under the exit sign. The elevator stopped.

Oh, come on, for God's sake! I thought, and it was like a shout in my head.

There was no need to shout. The whirring started again and I heard the cage grind down slowly and come to a faintly thudding stop, on the main floor. The sound was all I had to go by; there was no light in the cage. Whether there was anything else in it, I couldn't tell. It was one of those elevators that automatically returns to the main floor wherever you leave it.

Because I could hear it plainly enough, I concentrated on watching the stairway entrance. I could make out the framing all right and the exit sign gave enough light to outline the double door—two heavy wood panels, as I remembered, with small glass and wire mesh windows at eye level.

My eyes strained out of focus and I blinked and shook my head to clear them. When I found the doors again, something about them had changed. I hadn't seen it happen, but after a few seconds I accepted it; one of the big panels now stood open. So it was going to start now and I wondered what I would do.

It was black beyond the door. I couldn't see anything except a vague fuzzy glow around the exit sign. I stood by the pillar, watching, waiting for somebody to move, or merely to become visible. The elevator was silent. The whole damn place was entirely too damn silent. I felt around and got hold of a nearby lighting fixture on a stand; one of those three-unit brass lamps with a small, weighted base. I lifted and it came free of the stand. I got it well up over my shoulder and flung it hard toward the front door. It crashed on the floor, not far from the desk. I ducked to my right against the wall that enclosed the elevator shaft, got my shoulders against it and slid along toward the elevator door. It was a sliding type. I reached and got hold of the finger grip and pulled it open slowly. Flattened against the wall, I held it open, listening. After a while the secret of the elevator solved itself. There wasn't anybody in there. Couldn't be.

The happy thought gave me confidence. I let the door go and moved with it past the shaft and along a narrow aisle toward the stairway. Because of the different angle, or because I was closer, or because my eyes had adjusted themselves, I could see the open door. Also some of the floor area around it, well enough to see anybody step out there.

I managed to keep my feet silent moving over the concrete. My hand brushed against a table covered with small to medium-sized objects—cups and saucers, my fingers told me. I got hold of a cup and lobbed it into the center aisle toward the front. It made a good sound.

In the corner, along the wall beside the open door, were some packing cases. I made for them and ducked behind one, and now I could see the door opening just fine. There was a faint shuffling of feet. I held my breath for about thirty seconds, and a shadow slowly grew where there had been empty space. It was the older one, Davis. He was flat against the open door, edging his way out into the room an inch at a time, his neck twisted as he tried to find something. He had a gun in his hand, a good-sized one. The red glow made it gleam dully.

I leaned a little heavily on the packing case and it moved. I felt down underneath and found it was sitting on a dolly. I put both hands flat against the end of the case and waited. Davis inched out a little farther, then stopped, just inside the framing. I couldn't blame him for hesitating. For all he knew I was as well armed as he.

His head jerked upward. Suddenly he was conscious of being in the light. He slid on out into the room, then back along the wall into the shadow beside the door. I heard him take a deep breath. Then his hand snaked back, hooking around the edge of the door, and he tapped a couple of times with his fingers, a barely audible sound. I raised myself enough to get leverage in my ankles and waited for the other one to make his appearance.

He did it at about the same pace Davis had used, inching his way along the door panel. He had a gun too, a little smaller than the other; but his shadow cut a much more heroic figure than Davis'. He stopped for a few seconds, as Davis had stopped, then moved out from the door and into the clear. I went on waiting. I needed the two of them. I couldn't even see Davis any more, because of the shadow and the fact that Mr. America was in the way.

Then Davis moved out from the wall and nearer the other guy. It was my break that the only way they could communicate safely was by touch and gesture. In order to do this, they had to get close together.

They got that way, close enough, and their heads turned toward the front door. I rose on my haunches and got hold of the edges of the packing case. I rocked the dolly back once, to align the wheels, then pushed, driving it into them, going along with it, but sliding off at the doorway to roll clear toward the stairway.

I heard the impact, a violent explosion of curses as at least one of them went down, and then the shooting—wild and extravagant, in various directions. I was on my knees behind the open door, looking around it, when the shooting stopped. The packing case rolled back across the opening, banged the wall savagely and caromed off. Mr. America followed it, stooping low. He went on out of sight and Davis lurched into the arena, limping noticeably. He stopped under the red light and I gathered myself again and came around the edge of the door. It would have to go fast and right now, because they would be tipped to the fact that I had no arms.

Davis half turned. I hit him with my shoulder back of the knees, hard enough to spill him forward helplessly. His head hit the concrete and I felt sick. He didn't try to get up. I scrambled over him, feeling for his gun, but it had left him and I didn't have time to look for it. Mr. America had started shooting again from the protection of the packing case. I rolled over into a black place and came up against the legs of a table. It spilled with a cracking thud and I rolled away from it and let the big boy pump lead at it. He pumped quite a lot. Then I heard the fatal click and knew his string had run out.

I got up fast then and headed for the packing case. I was short of it when he rose up from behind it and slashed at my head with, the pistol. I kicked the case at him and he stumbled but stayed on his feet. He grabbed the case with both hands and swung it away from him, then charged me with the pistol. He had a long reach and I had to duck blindly. Doing it, I lost my balance and fell into him. He brought the thing down and it glanced off my hip bone. It hurt.

I got my arms around his thighs and brought him down, but he wouldn't let go of the gun. He kept catching me with it, on the legs, the back. I drew my head in as far as possible, slid down his legs and got one of his feet in both hands. When I twisted it, he gave in and rolled over. I went for his gun hand and got hold of it, but he was strong as a big ape and I couldn't break his grip.

He surged under me, rolling, and I fell clear and slid across the floor into Davis. It was like hitting a bag of flour. My knees were bruised from the concrete and my right hand was numb. Mr. America came charging at me and I rolled into his legs and let him fall on Davis. I got up and turned. The big guy started up and I kicked him in the ribs, then came down with both hands on the back of his neck. He sagged and I thought I had him, but he started up again, swinging at me with the pistol. When I jumped back, the swing carried him all the way and he went down on one shoulder. I kicked at his wrist and he let go of the gun. I kicked that out of the way. I got hold of his coat and pulled him up into position and started belting him on the chin. It took four belts to do it, but he finally went out and stayed down.

I found my way to the front desk and turned on the light. It took about two minutes of searching to find Davis' gun. When I checked it, it was in working condition and loaded. I carried it over to where I had left Hayes on the davenport. He looked up at me through that horrible slit.

"Can you make it over here?" I asked, jerking my head toward the stairway.

He nodded and started up. I gave him a hand. He leaned on me for a few steps, then straightened up and he was doing all right. I took him over there, showed him the two guys on the floor, and found a place for him to sit. I gave him the gun.

"In case they come around," I said, "before I get back."

He nodded.

"I'll get Dorothy now," I said.

He nodded again. I left him there and went to the elevator.

* * * *

There was a dim light in the small reception room on the ninth floor. Somebody had pulled the cleaver out of the door and laid it on the receptionist's desk. A nice greeting for her, come morning.

Brophy's big office was lighted and empty. I could hear voices in the apartment beyond: his, low and grating; then hers, a little strident.

"I wish you'd stop it now," she said. "Somebody's coming. I heard the elevator."

"Just the boys," Brophy said. "That detective friend of yours was quite a nuisance."

"I don't care. Just stop. Just stop talking like that."

"You're my wife," Brophy said with some surprise. "I got a right to chew you out a little."

One of the things about guys like Brophy—they just can't imagine how they could ever lose. That's not too bad as a trait, but it's likely to lead to disillusionment. It was going to be a big fat pleasure to disillusion Brophy.

When I walked into the apartment, Dorothy Stanhope was pacing back and forth in front of that high window. Brophy was lying on his back on the studio couch, in his shirtsleeves, smoking a cigarette. Dorothy's back was turned at the moment and she didn't bother to look around right away. Brophy saw me, though, and his cigarette hovered somewhere over his chest, halted en route to his mouth. His shrewd eyes slid to Dorothy, then to the window, finally to a night stand beside the couch and eventually again to me. It was about then that Dorothy turned in her pacing and saw me for the first time.

"Mac—"

Her right hand went up and plucked at something on her shoulder.

"Hi," I said, watching Brophy. "I guess we can go now, if you're ready."

"Watch it, bulldog," Brophy grated.

He hadn't moved, except in the quiet subtle way a man moves when he pulls his muscles together and tries to figure out a standby philosophy to carry him through a bad time.

"Miss Stanhope—?" I suggested, indicating the door.

She stood there. Brophy snuffed out his cigarette on the night stand. She got started then and Brophy tightened.

"Don't go, kid," he warned.

She stopped and her eyes chased mine.

"Foster—?" she said.

"He'll be all right," I said. "He's downstairs."

Brophy was up on his elbows.

"Don't go!" he barked.

He was lean, craggy, hard. I had had enough of him. I stepped to one side, into the room, to get her out from between us.

"You want to fight for her?" I said to him. "Come on."

In a way he wanted to, but mostly he didn't. His eyes got that look and he bunched, his lips thinned out, and for about a minute he might have been ready to fly at me. But then he lost the push; the fight look went away and he wasn't looking at me or at her any more, or at anything special except whatever it was inside himself.

So I nodded to Miss Stanhope and she went out. She didn't look back that I know of. I stayed there until I knew she had had time to make the elevator. Then I turned my back on Brophy and walked away. It was pretty foolish. I ought to have died then, but I didn't. Maybe somebody had been watching after all.

CHAPTER TWENTY-ONE

Downstairs I called an ambulance for Hayes and while we waited for it, I frisked Brophy's two sullen lieutenants for additional weapons, got them on their feet and into the elevator and on their way upstairs. Dorothy Stanhope went with Hayes in the ambulance. She had some things to say to me, but I don't remember what they were, though I was pleased at the time to hear them. After that, there was the brief, cold walk to my car, that had a parking ticket on it for standing in the loading zone.

* * * *

In the office I sat down at my desk and took a bottle out of the drawer and set it up where I could look at it.

I decided it didn't look good. I put it away and looked at the telephone for a while. It was no work of art, but it had some use. I looked up a number, pulled the thing off the hook and dialed. It rang only twice before she answered, so I guessed she had just come off duty.

"Oh—hi!" she said, with that upward lilt in her happy little voice. "How are you feeling?"

"I'm not sure."

"Well—can I do anything for you—nurse-wise?"

"Maybe. Are you dressed?"

"That's none of your business."

"I'll buy you a drink."

"Everything's closed up."

"My desk isn't closed."

"Well, if you really need—"

"I really need."

I hung up. She would come. It was her pattern. She was conditioned to service.

Ten minutes passed before I heard her light knock. I opened the door and she came in, wearing a light topcoat over her uniform, complete to little cap and those cotton hose they wear.

"Just in case," she said, "somebody might notice. I could say I'm on a call."

I closed the door.

"I love you," I said.

"Don't say that."

"All right. Do you really want a drink?"

"No, thanks."

"Neither do I."

There was one of those awkward little pauses. After a minute she took off her cap and the topcoat and put them on the couch and sat down beside them with her hands in her lap.

"Thanks for calling Donovan," I said. "You probably saved my life."

"Was it the right thing to do?"

"Yes, baby."

Another pause.

"Did you have a hard night?" I asked.

"Not especially. No emergencies tonight."

I sat down beside her on the couch and she sat very still, looking at her hands in her lap; and her beautiful red hair was a mass of random ringlets on her head.

"Would it be all right if I run my fingers through your hair?" I said.

She looked at me.

"Well—sure—I guess so—"

It was soft and resilient and sprang quickly into place after I had ruffled it.

"Real hair," I said.

She laughed.

"Yup," she said. "It's all mine."

She laid her head on my shoulder and I could feel her hair against my neck.

"You're a lucky girl," I said.

"Because I have hair? Everybody has hair."

"I knew a girl who hadn't."

She straightened and moved her head back to stare at me.

"That would be awful! You mean she was bald?"

"It was pretty awful."

We sat there. I ran my hand through her hair for quite a long time and she sat patiently, submissive, acquiescent. She didn't ask me to tell her about the girl with no hair and I never did.

I told Donovan, some time later. I don't think he believed me, but maybe he did. He wouldn't have given it too much time. Donovan's vocation keeps him pretty busy.